The
Christmas
Charm

Deanna Lynn Sletten

Novels by

Deanna Lynn Sletten

WOMEN'S FICTION

The Secrets We Carry

The Ones We Leave Behind

The Women of Great Heron Lake

Miss Etta

Night Music

One Wrong Turn

Finding Libbie

Maggie's Turn

Summer of the Loon

Memories

Widow, Virgin, Whore

MURDER/MYSTERY

Rachel Emery Series

The Truth About Rachel

Death Becomes You

ROMANCE

Destination Wedding

Sara's Promise

Lake Harriet Series

Under the Apple Blossoms

Chasing Bailey

As the Snow Fell

Walking Sam

Kiss a Cowboy Series

Kiss a Cowboy

A Kiss for Colt

Kissing Carly

YOUNG ADULT

Outlaw Heroes

The
Christmas
Charm

CHAPTER ONE

Christmas Eve 1959

June Elden waited anxiously for her husband to come home from his long day of work at his father's dairy farm. She'd returned home from her own part-time job at the local dime-store earlier in the day and baked sugar cookies and stuffed a chicken for dinner. Now, she waited eagerly for their first Christmas as a married couple to begin.

For the hundredth time, June walked around their tiny apartment, fluffing the sofa pillows and straightening the cushion on the old rocker her father had given her, making sure that everything was tidy and nice. They lived above the old furniture store in downtown Redmond in a one-bedroom space with a small sitting area and an even smaller kitchen, but June didn't mind. At nineteen-years-old, she was with the man she adored and loved their life together.

The door suddenly burst open, and with it came a rush of crisp air as the Minnesota winter followed Patrick inside.

"Juni? Juni-bug? Are you here?" Patrick called with a grin on his face and a glint in his brown eyes.

June ran to the door, her dark pony-tail swinging as she moved, and wrapped her arms around her husband. "Of course, I'm here," she said, hugging him close. He smelled of cows, straw, and damp wool, but she didn't mind. June gazed up at him expectantly. "Did you bring it?"

"You mean this?" Patrick reached outside and pulled hard on something heavy. Suddenly, the room filled with the smell of fresh pine.

"Oh, it's here!" June clapped her hands together and jumped with glee. Together, they moved the heavy spruce tree into the tiny living room and closed the door against the freezing air. "I have a tree stand right over here," June said. She stopped suddenly and bit her lip. "I hope you don't mind. I know we're saving every penny so you can open your own store someday. But I bought it and a few ornaments at the dime store today."

Patrick slipped off his plaid coat, hung it on the hook by the door, and walked over to hug his bride. "Of course, I don't mind," he said gently. "We can't have a tree without some sparkle, now, can we?"

The couple worked together to place the tree in the stand and set it up in the corner. Then they let it sit while June served dinner on the little card table that functioned as a dining set.

"Dinner smells delicious," Patrick said, sitting down. "How lucky I am to have married such a great cook."

June smiled at him as they served up. Being the only girl in her family, she'd had no choice but to learn to cook for her father and brother after her mother had died when June was twelve. She actually hadn't minded it, though. June enjoyed cooking new dishes and baking treats.

They filled up on roasted chicken, stuffing, carrots, and rolls, then each enjoyed one of her holiday cookies. Patrick pushed away from the table and sat back after sipping his coffee. "I think I'm too full to move," he said.

"But we have to decorate the tree," June said, suddenly worried. She knew he worked long hours at his father's farm and had hoped he wouldn't be too tired to help her decorate.

Patrick grinned. He unfolded his tall body from the small chair, stood, and stretched. His long legs and arms enabled him to touch the ceiling. "I'm never too tired to celebrate Christmas," he said.

June rushed to wrap up the leftovers and stack the dishes in the sink. As she did, Patrick pulled a long string of colorful big-bulbed lights out of a box and began clipping them to the tree.

"I'm glad my mom had an extra set of tree lights," he said as he placed them. "They'll look great with your new ornaments."

June moved quickly to the living room, her full skirt swishing around her knees. "They're going to look lovely," she said excitedly.

Once the lights were on, June carefully opened the boxes of mercery-glass ornaments, and they took turns placing them on the tree. There weren't many, but they looked beautiful as they shimmered in the light.

"Oh!" June stared at the tree, dismayed. "I forgot to get a tree topper."

Patrick studied the tree that nearly touched the ceiling. "I think it'll be fine without one this year," he said. "You can buy one on sale after the holidays, and we'll have something new to put on the tree next year."

June nodded. "Yes. Next year." She smiled over at Patrick. "We have a lifetime to fill our Christmas trees with memories."

Patrick hugged her close.

June made hot chocolate, and they turned out the lights and sat on the sofa, admiring their handiwork. She loved how cozy their apartment was with only the tree lights illuminating it.

"Should we open presents tonight?" Patrick asked. "Just us alone? Tomorrow we'll be at my parents' house, and it'll be chaos."

June nodded. "Oh, yes. Let's." She hurried to their bedroom, pulled a box out from under the bed, and then placed it under the tree.

"For me?" Patrick said playfully as they both kneeled beside the tree.

"Silly. Open it," June said.

Patrick picked up the box and shook it. Then he placed it to his ear and shook it again. "A puppy?" he asked.

June laughed. "That would be a very small puppy."

"Hm. A tie?" he teased.

"Why on earth would you need another tie? So you could dress up for the dairy cows?"

"Well, it's too small to be a brand-new car," he said.

"Just open it, silly," June told him.

Patrick ripped off the red Santa paper with the enthusiasm of a child and then lifted the box lid. Inside lay a thick pair of suede gloves with warm fur lining. "These are great," he said, slipping them onto his large hands. "And so warm. I love them."

"Do you? Really? I know they're practical, but you needed a warm pair of work gloves," June said, worrying her lower lip with her teeth.

Patrick leaned over and kissed her sweetly on the cheek. "I love them. I really do. And I need them. No more frozen hands." He grinned.

This brought a smile to June's face.

"Now, it's your turn," Patrick said. "But first, you have to find it."

"What?" June glanced around. "You hid it?"

"Yep. But I'll give you a hint. It's somewhere in the tree."

"In the tree?" June frowned. She stood and began searching the tree branches. "What kind of gift can you hide in a tree?" she asked.

"A really good one," he teased.

June searched the tree, then finally looked around toward the back. "I found it!" she said gleefully. Carefully, June picked up the small, wrapped box that sat on a branch. She came to sit beside Patrick on the floor again, staring at the box.

"What could it be?" she asked.

"You'll have to open it to see," Patrick said.

June shook the box. "It makes a jingling sound. Is it a bell?"

Patrick laughed. "Are you a cat?"

June giggled. "Is it the tiniest pair of gloves ever?"

"Maybe for a tiny fairy princess," Patrick said. "Open it."

June couldn't contain her curiosity any longer. She carefully unwrapped the pretty silver paper and opened the small box. Inside was another box—a red velvet one that looked like a jewelry box. Her expression grew serious.

"Oh, Patrick. You didn't spend a lot of money on me, did you?" she asked, feeling guilty.

"It's Christmas, Juni-bug. Can't I spoil you once a year?" Patrick said sweetly.

Growing excited, June lifted the lid. Sitting on red velvet was a white-gold star charm on a chain. As she moved the box in the light, it twinkled. "Oh, it's beautiful," she said, looking up into Patrick's eyes. "I love it."

He grinned. "Try it on."

She lifted it out of the box and held it in her hand. It was quite thick and heavy for so small a charm. Unclasping the chain, she placed it around her neck, then smiled at Patrick. "I love it. I really do. But it's so expensive," she said.

"You're worth every cent to me," her husband said, drawing closer. "I wanted to give you something nice for our first Christmas. Something that would remind you of how happy we are every time you wear it for years to come. Something special you can hand down to our daughter, and she can hand down to her daughter. I love you, Juni. Our first Christmas will always be our most special one."

Tears filled June's eyes as she pulled Patrick close. "I'm so happy," she whispered in his ear.

He kissed her, and they sat together in each other's arms until the church bells rang at midnight, announcing Christmas Day.

CHAPTER TWO

December 21, 2022

Jessica Paxton pulled her Toyota Highlander into her home-town just as the clock on the dash struck four. She'd left her office in Minneapolis exactly at noon and, after leaving the city behind, drove the backroads of western Minnesota to the middle of nowhere. Redmond. A town of roughly twelve hundred people, sitting on a one-mile square plot of land in the middle of Minnesota farm country.

After passing the large grain bins that sat beside the rail-road tracks, Jess drove five blocks down and turned right. Nothing had changed in the three years since she'd visited. Or, in the eighteen years since she'd left for college. She passed the familiar Dairy Queen, the city baseball fields, the Farmers Insurance building, and even the little Jubilee grocery store. No—nothing had changed.

When she reached Sixth Avenue, the old Victorian house on the corner loomed large. Jess passed the driveway that led to the garage and turned the corner before pulling alongside a blue minivan in the other driveway of the stately home. Putting the car in park and shutting it off, Jessica sat there and sighed. She was home. So why did she dread walking inside?

The house looked the same—well kept up and inviting. Snow covered the rooftop, and Christmas lights lined the porch roof, columns, and lower windows. More lights were placed on the perfect little pine tree in the front yard and wrapped up the trunk of the old oak tree. Once it grew dark, the house would look like a fairy tale come alive. But like all fairy tales, there were dark undertones that seeped along the edges.

Sighing again, Jess slid her shoulder-length brown hair behind her ears, forced herself to step out of her car, and grabbed her suitcase from the back. Glancing up and down the tree-lined street, she studied the neighborhood of old homes. Nearly every house in this town had been built between 1896 and 1940. There were immaculate homes alongside run-down ones. She glanced over at the house next door and smiled, remembering the boy who'd lived there and how they'd run back and forth between the houses. Turning, she saw the park that was kitty-corner to the house, a stretch of land covered in snow with tall trees and play equipment on the other end. A public pool sat covered, fenced-in, and closed for the winter. She remembered the summer she and the neighbor boy, Jay, worked as lifeguards at the pool, turning golden brown from sitting in the hot sun day after day.

"Are you going to stand in the freezing cold all day or come inside?" a voice called to her from the front porch.

Jess turned her head and smiled when she saw her baby sister, Skyler. The petite mother of two didn't look her full age of thirty years old. She looked more like a sixteen-year-old girl waiting for her older sister to let her drive her car. Jess walked up to the porch and hugged her.

"I'm so glad you came," Skyler squealed, smiling wide as she pulled away. "Come inside before we freeze."

They walked through the antique door with the oval, stained-glass window into the living room. Jess glanced around. Everything was the same. The large cushy sofa and loveseat, her father's recliner, and her grandmother's wooden rocking chair with a cushion on the seat. A rug sat under the coffee table over the original oak flooring her grandparents had restored decades before. Since her grandmother's death three years ago, her mother hadn't changed a thing. But when her eyes fell on the Christmas tree in the corner, Jess frowned.

"Is that a fake tree?" she asked incredulously. "Where's the real tree we always have? And those aren't Grandma's antique ornaments." She turned to her sister. "What's going on?"

"Mom hasn't put up a real tree with Grandma's ornaments since she passed," Skyler said in a hushed voice. "It's best if you don't say anything, okay?"

The sound of a car pulling into the garage on the other side of the house caught their attention.

"That's mom coming home from the hardware store," Skyler said. "I have to run. I need to pick up the kids from the babysitter and lock up the shop. We're all meeting at The Pier for dinner tonight, so I'll see you there." She turned to head out the door, but Jessica followed her.

"The Pier? The old pub? I thought that was closed," Jess said.

Skyler looked puzzled. "What other pier would I mean? A new owner took over, and it's a great place to eat."

"Wait. You're leaving me here all alone with mom?"

Skyler laughed. "You're a big girl. You'll be fine. Dad will be home shortly, and we'll all be at The Pier later. I really have to go." She gave her a grin. "Have fun."

Jess watched Skyler close the door with a sinking heart. She hadn't expected to face her mother—alone—so soon. Turning back toward the kitchen, she heard someone moving around. Jess walked past the farm-style dining room table and was about to push on the kitchen's swinging door when it suddenly opened toward her. She jumped back before it could hit her.

"Oh. You're actually here." Florence Paxton stood there, staring at her second-eldest child.

"Hi, Mom." Jess tried to sound enthusiastic, but her words fell flat. The two studied each other for a moment. In three years, her mother hadn't changed much except for a little more gray in her dark brown hair. Her mother was the same height as Skyler, about two inches shorter than Jess, and had put on a few extra pounds but was by no means overweight. But her blue eyes still had the same piercing stare that Jess remembered so well.

"Well, I'm glad you made it," Florence said, giving her a cursory hug and then stepping around her to set paperwork on the rolltop desk on the opposite side of the living room. For as long as Jess could remember, her mother had done the bookkeeping for the hardware store. Where once she'd worked with large ledger books, she now used a computer that sat on the desk.

"Me, too," Jess said, feeling uneasy. Making small talk with her mother was never easy. "So, I guess I'll take my suitcase upstairs."

"Did Skyler tell you we're having dinner at The Pier?" her mother asked.

"Yes."

"Good." Florence looked Jess up and down. "You may want

to dress it down a little for around here. People will think you're going to a funeral in that suit you're wearing."

Jess looked down at her black and white pinstripe suit and black heels. She'd come directly from work and hadn't bothered to change. Working in a law office as a divorce attorney, Jess was used to dressing nice. "Yeah. I'll change into jeans or something," she told her mother.

"Good. You know where your room is. It's all ready for you. Be ready to leave the house by five." Florence turned and walked back into the kitchen.

"Nice to see you too, Mom," Jess mumbled as she lifted her suitcase and headed up the narrow staircase across from the kitchen.

Once upstairs, Jess walked down the hallway past Skyler's old room and turned left into what used to be her bedroom. She stopped in the doorframe and sighed. Again, nothing had changed. The wallpaper was still the same cream with pink roses, and the twin beds sat across from each other with a nightstand in-between. The white dresser sat opposite from the beds with two 8x10 picture frames, one on each side. One photo was Jess's senior portrait, and the other was of Elaina, her older sister.

Jess stepped into the room, set her suitcase down, then lifted Elaina's picture off the desk. Elaina was the perfect one—tall, slender, athletic, smart—the entire package. She was chosen valedictorian in her class and had earned a full academic scholarship at the University of California, Berkeley. Elaina loved science and chemistry and couldn't wait to go away to college. But it never happened. She died before she even had a chance to graduate high school.

Jess closed her eyes and remembered the day her sister

died. Elaina had been so full of life. She was wearing cut-off jean shorts, sneakers, and a tank top because there'd been an unexpected hot spell that weekend. She was flushed from her tense conversation with their mother and had run out of the kitchen and grabbed Jess's hand. "Come on, Jess. Let's go for a drive." They'd slipped into her yellow Ford Mustang, blasted the stereo, and driven off.

Opening her eyes, Jess willed herself to stop the story there. It was such a great memory until the worst happened.

Setting Elaina's photo back on the dresser, Jess placed her suitcase on her sister's bed and began unpacking. She was going to be here until Monday, so she'd brought enough clothes to last for five days. Five long days. Already, she wasn't sure she was going to last that long.

* * *

Jess had just finished changing into jeans, a sweater, and fleece-lined boots when she heard her father's voice downstairs. Smiling, she glanced quickly in the mirror to smooth her hair, then hurried down the stairs.

"Dad!" she said excitedly, and he turned and opened his arms.

"There's my best girl." He gave her a warm bear hug. "It's been too long."

"It has," Jess said, wrapping her arms around his broad build. Except for his dark hair turning silver, her father had hardly changed over the years. He was built sturdy but not fat. His high energy kept his weight in check. His brown eyes were warm and accessible, and his smile touched the heart of even the grumpiest person in the room.

"You look wonderful!" Thomas said, studying his daughter. "I guess life in the big city agrees with you."

Jess smiled. "It's not too bad, even with a stressful job."

"How's that townhouse of yours? Are you in need of any repairs?"

Jess laughed. "You don't need a reason to visit, Dad. You can come anytime. But I'm sure there's something you could fix or remodel if you wanted to."

"The last thing that man needs is more work," Florence said gruffly, entering the living room. "He already puts in too many hours at the hardware store."

Jess pulled away from her father, the mood now dampened.

"Ah, Flo, dear," Thomas said heartily. "You know I always have time for my daughters."

Florence grunted as she walked to the hall closet and grabbed her coat. "Aren't you going to wear a coat?" she asked Jess over her shoulder.

"I left my coat upstairs," Jess said, heading for the staircase. Before she reached it, another big voice boomed in the room.

"I heard my big sister is home!"

Jess turned and grinned at Richard as he and his wife, Mandy, entered through the front door. "You don't look like my little brother anymore," she said gleefully as he pulled her into a hug. Rick was big like her father except with a lot of added weight. His dark hair was cut short, but he had a thick, well-kept beard covering his face. He had played football in high school, but he was just a big teddy bear.

"I'll remind you that you're two years older than me," he teased. "You're getting old!"

Jess laughed. "I am, but you're right behind me," she said. "Hi, Mandy, how's it going?" She hugged her sister-in-law.

She'd known Mandy for years because she and Rick had been childhood sweethearts. She truly was like another sister.

"I'm good," Mandy said.

"How's the shop doing?" Jess inquired. Mandy opened a hair salon five years ago next door to Skyler's boutique. Granted, in a little town like Redmond, all the stores were close together.

"It's doing great. I'm busy all the time. I suppose you wouldn't want to give up being a lawyer and become a hairstylist. I could use another one in the shop." Mandy grinned.

"No one wants me to cut their hair," Jess said. "I like the pink stripe, by the way." Mandy's long dark hair generally had a pink, purple, or red stripe in it, depending on her mood.

"Thanks."

"I don't know why you girls want unnatural colors in your hair," Florence said from behind Jess. "But I do admit it suits Mandy."

The group all stared at each other and stopped talking.

"Here." Florence pushed an old color-block winter coat into Jess's arms. "Wear this. We're going to be late."

Jess stared down at her junior high jacket. "I doubt this will fit."

"It'll fit. You're as thin as ever. Let's go." Florence led the way. Thomas followed his wife out the door as Jess tried the jacket on. Surprisingly, it fit.

"Stylin," Mandy said, chuckling. Jess shrugged and followed everyone out the door.

Jess rode with her parents in her dad's old hardware store SUV while Rick and Mandy followed behind them. Within minutes, they were across town, where the streets ended, and the lake began.

Lake Redmond was an oasis in the middle of corn country.

It was large and deep for a lake in their area. A natural spring and a tiny creek kept it fed with clear, cold water. Houses were built around the lake—many new and expensive homes.

They pulled into the parking lot next to The Pier. It was an old log building that had once been a local liquor store and then a restaurant before it was remodeled and became a bar and restaurant in the 1990s. After the last owners retired, it sat empty for a few years, but now it was lit up and busy as only a small-town restaurant—one of only three—could be.

Jess glanced around as she followed everyone toward the open front porch. Many houses behind them were lit brightly with Christmas lights, as were several homes around the lake. Even at a distance, she saw white or colorful lights outlining rooftops and windows. The air was crisp, and the snow crunched under her boots. It was nothing like the suburb of Golden Valley where she lived or Minneapolis where she worked. Those places were busy, and the snow turned dirty very quickly. Here, everything was slow, peaceful, and still.

Her dad held the door open as Jess followed the group inside. The lights were turned low, and the noise level was slightly high. People were sitting at tables all around, enjoying a beer and a burger, wings, or hot sandwich. The place had been remodeled since Jess had last been there, making it more open, with the bar now a large circle in the middle. Wood beams were exposed in the tall ceiling, and a stone fireplace had a crackling fire at one end. In the back of the room were pool and foosball tables. Jess smiled. She and her friends had played both of those games for hours on end in high school.

"Over here," Skyler called, waving them toward the fireplace. She sat at a long, farmhouse-style table with her husband Christopher and their two children, Aaron and Kaylie.

"Oh, my goodness. You're both so big!" Jess exclaimed as she sat next to Skyler and the kids on a bench seat. Aaron was five years old, and Kaylie was three. Both were blond and blue-eyed with sweet cherub faces.

"Well, you haven't seen them since Kaylie was a baby," Florence said, sitting across the table from Skyler.

Jess let out a soft sigh but forced a smile on her lips. "I'm seeing them now, and they're both adorable," she said.

Kaylie scooched closer to her mother, but Aaron looked interested in Jess.

"Don't mind Kaylie; she's a little shy," Skyler told Jess. "She'll warm up to you by Christmas."

Jess asked Aaron about the toy truck in his hand, and he quickly explained to her exactly what make and model it was. It wasn't long before he was chatting up a storm with his aunt.

"That kid loves his cars and trucks," Chris said, smiling over at Jess. "So, how's the divorce business? Going strong, I'll bet."

Jess looked up at Skyler's husband and tried not to cringe. He'd always seemed a little too slick to her. Chris had left town for college and come back very full of himself. He sold crop insurance like his father and also dabbled in real estate. But with his perfectly combed sandy-blond hair and fake smile, he always seemed like he was conning something. Jess had no idea what Skyler had ever seen in him.

"Divorce is a never-ending business," Jess answered. "People have a knack for marrying the wrong person."

"I think it would be depressing, helping people dissolve their marriages," Skyler said. "But I guess someone has to do it."

Jess shrugged.

A waitress came over, passed around menus, and took the groups' drink orders. Jess opted for a soda since the kids were there and was a little surprised when Chris ordered a whiskey sour. She hoped Skyler would be the one driving them home.

"So, what's good here?" Jess asked, scanning the menu. It was typical bar food—burgers, chicken strips, sandwiches. Her dad suggested a burger, Rick said the barbecue wings were great, and Skyler suggested the club wrap. Jess decided to go with Skyler's suggestion and ordered that when the waitress returned.

"This place is really busy," Jess said to no one in particular. "The new owners must be pleased with how well it's doing."

Skyler grinned. "Owner—singular. He's from here and single."

"Sky," Florence said in a warning tone. "Leave it be."

Skyler's eyes sparkled mischievously. "He's the guy pouring drinks behind the bar," she told Jess.

Jess looked at the bar, which was bustling with waitresses and bartenders. Her eyes suddenly locked with a tall, sandy blond-haired man who looked in need of a haircut. The face was older than she remembered, but she knew those blue eyes. She'd gazed into them thousands of times throughout her life and especially while they'd dated in high school.

"Jay?"

It was as if he'd heard her all the way across the room. He smiled, nodded, then headed toward their table.

CHAPTER THREE

Christmas Eve 1964

June sat on the second-hand sofa her in-laws had given them, feeding a bottle to her three-month-old daughter. She snuggled little Florence close, still in awe of how beautiful she was. Soon, Patrick would be home with their Christmas tree, and they'd decorate it while little Flori slept.

They'd continued the tradition of decorating their tree every Christmas Eve since they'd married. Then they would spend Christmas day with Pat's parents and the family. Her own father had sold his gas station and moved to Arizona, where he said the warm weather helped his arthritis feel better. He'd met a woman and remarried. Her brother had joined the Army and seemed fine with living a nomad lifestyle. June worried about him, though. There was a conflict beginning in a small country named Vietnam, and it seemed to be intensifying. She'd heard about it on the radio. June hoped her brother wouldn't be sent there.

"I'm home," Pat sang out as he opened the door and then immediately shushed himself when he saw the baby asleep in

June's arms. "I'll bring in the tree after you put her down," he whispered. After closing the door and taking off his snowy boots and heavy coat, Pat sat on the sofa next to his wife. "She's a doll," he said lovingly. "We did good."

June smiled. She knew Pat was just as excited about their baby as she was. After three miscarriages, they'd begun to believe they might never be able to have children. That had torn June apart. Being a parent was something she'd always wanted. But then she became pregnant with their little girl, and she'd been a fighter. Despite several scares and June having to rest the last two months of her pregnancy, Flori had been born—a healthy, pudgy eight-and-a-half-pound baby. She was the most precious gift June and Pat could ever have hoped for.

June carried the baby to her crib in their bedroom and laid her down. They were outgrowing their little apartment, but the couple had no choice but to stay. They'd been saving every penny so Pat could open his own business and were hopeful their dream might come true in the next year. After that, they could save for a house.

By the time June had reentered the living room, Pat had pulled the large pine tree inside and was putting the stand on it. Together, they lifted the tree and set it in the corner by the window. After making sure it was straight, June filled the pan with water, and Pat went to work clipping the lights on.

Over the past few years, June had managed to buy a tree topper and more ornaments when they were on sale. They'd added two more strings of lights as well. Now that she no longer worked at the dime store, they had to be even thriftier with their money.

June pulled the roast out of the oven and served it on the laminate table she'd found at a garage sale. The chair pads had a few holes, but otherwise, it was a nice upgrade from their old card table. June turned the radio on to listen to Christmas music while they ate.

"Ah. I'm hungry," Pat said as he sat down to eat. He placed a pile of roast beef, carrots, and mashed potatoes on his plate. Then covered it all in gravy.

"Gravy on your carrots!" June asked.

"Gravy's good on everything," he said, smiling.

"How was your day at work?" June asked. She knew how hard he worked at the dairy farm, but he never complained.

"The same. Always the same. I'll be so glad when I can finally do something else for a living," Pat said.

June reached over and patted his hand. "We're getting closer, dear. Maybe next year will be our year."

Pat smiled at her. "Yes. Let's hope. I've been studying up on what I'll need to know to run a business, and I'm looking into the costs. I think we could rent that little corner store downtown and fill it with merchandise by next year. As long as no one else rents that space."

"I highly doubt anyone will," June said. "Businesses are closing right now, not opening." She bit her lip. "I hope the town isn't dying."

"Things will be fine, Juni-bug. Farmers need tools, and homeowners need supplies to fix their homes. A hardware store is just what this little town needs. Otherwise, everyone has to drive over an hour to Watertown for supplies."

June nodded. He was right. Having the items in town that people needed most would bring in business.

After dinner, June washed the dishes while Pat finished putting lights on the tree. Then she joined him in decorating the tree with the beautiful ornaments she'd collected over the past few years. Finally, they both sat back on the sofa and admired their handiwork. The ornaments twinkled under the tree lights.

"Another beautiful tree," Pat said, smiling over at June. He gazed at her a moment, then frowned.

"What's wrong?" June asked.

"Where's your Christmas charm necklace?"

June reached up instinctively and then remembered. "I forgot to put it on today," she said, relieved it wasn't lost. "Besides, Flori pulls on it, and I'm afraid she'll break the chain."

"But it's not Christmas until you wear your necklace," Pat said.

June laughed. "I'll get it." She walked softly into their room so as not to wake Flori. She picked up the necklace from her small jewelry box and brought it to the living room.

"Here, let me help you," Pat said. June handed him the necklace and turned, pulling her hair aside. Pat clasped the chain, then placed a sweet kiss on the nape of her neck. "There. Everything is as it should be," he said softly.

They snuggled on the sofa, content with their lives. They had agreed not to buy gifts for each other that year since money was tight, and they both agreed that Flori was the best gift of all.

"We have a good life," June said, sighing.

"We do," Pat said, wrapping his arm around her shoulders. "And it will only get better as each year goes by."

June looked up at her husband, her deep love for him obvious. "Merry Christmas," she said.

"Merry Christmas, Juni-bug," he said. Then kissed her sweetly on the lips.

CHAPTER FOUR

2022

Jess watched as Jay Michael Tannon approached their table. He was no longer the lanky teen she remembered before she left town for college. He'd filled out quite nicely, and his face had become more angular with age. But it was those blue eyes that grabbed her—they twinkled like Christmas lights as he drew near.

"Well, I'll be. Skyler said you were coming home, but I wasn't going to believe it until I saw it," Jay said, smiling warmly at Jess.

Jess sat silent, not knowing what to do as the entire table of relatives stared at her, waiting for her response. She finally stood and gave Jay an awkward hug. "No one told me you owned this place. It's great seeing you." She tried to sound lighthearted. The truth was, she was completely taken aback. She hadn't seen Jay since the day they'd parted when she'd left for college. And that hadn't been a happy ending.

"Yeah, it's a long story, but I'm back home. I'm even living in my childhood house right next door to you. We'll have to get together while you're here and rehash old times." Jay smiled, but this time it didn't go up to his eyes.

"Yeah, that'd be great," Jess said.

"Well, I'd better get back to work. It's busy tonight. Enjoy your meal." Jay smiled at everyone at the table and then headed back to the bar.

"I always liked Jay," Florence said pointedly as Jess sat down. "I'm glad he came home."

Jess let that comment pass as she glared at Skyler for not warning her.

After they'd all eaten, everyone went back to the house. Jess had hoped she could hide in her room for the rest of the evening, but she didn't want to be rude. She loved sitting around and talking with her siblings, but her mother had a way of making everyone feel awkward.

The kids ran to the closet under the stairs to pull out toys Florence kept there as the adults sat in the living room and chatted. Thomas and Rick talked about the hardware store while Chris sat off to the side, looking bored. Florence had chosen the old wooden rocking chair to sit in, and Skyler and Jess were on the sofa. Mandy sat on the floor despite Florence telling her she should sit on the loveseat.

"You know me, Mom," Mandy said. "I'm comfortable anywhere."

Her comment made Jess smile. That was what she loved about Mandy. She'd always been easy to get along with and never had a bad word to say about anyone. She'd fit perfectly into the family, unlike Chris, who always seemed like he'd rather be somewhere else.

"So, why don't you have a real tree this year?" Jess asked, looking around at everyone. "Don't you miss the pine smell?"

Everyone grew quiet, and their eyes darted toward Florence. "Real trees are so messy. And dangerous," Florence said. "This tree is easier."

"What about Grandma's ornaments?" Jess asked.

Her mother's face tightened. "They're old and fragile. I'd hate to break them. New traditions aren't so bad, are they?" She stared hard at Jess.

Jess was about to reply when Skyler interrupted. "You should come by the boutique tomorrow, and we can go to lunch," she said pointedly to Jess. "I've gotten in so many beautiful items for Christmas."

The conversation around the room started up again. Florence stood to get coffee and cookies and headed into the kitchen. Jess sighed. Nothing had changed around here. Everyone was still walking on eggshells around her mother. And without her beloved grandma here as a buffer, it was even more difficult.

Mandy went into the kitchen to help Florence, so Jess followed her. She knew her mother would be nice with Mandy around. Jess stacked homemade Christmas cookies on a plate while Mandy got the coffee tray ready for Florence. When they returned to the living room, the kids ran over to join them for a cookie.

Jess watched everyone as they enjoyed their cookies and coffee. Her mother was really good with the grandchildren. She liked seeing that. It hadn't been that way when she and her siblings had been children. They'd been expected to be perfect little people who did well in school and never got into trouble. For Elaina and Jess, doing well in school had come naturally, although Jess did work hard at it. For Rick, it had been a struggle. Florence often chided him for not paying enough attention to his schoolwork and too much time on sports. Somehow Skyler, being the youngest and cutest, had been given a pass on everything. She'd done okay in school, as far as Jess knew, and had been a cheerleader and prom queen, but Florence hadn't put pressure on her to be perfect. Jess envied Skyler for that. She wondered if things would have been different for her and Elaina if her mother had been more relaxed with them, too.

Rick and Mandy were the first to say goodnight and leave, and then Skyler reluctantly got up and helped the kids with their coats.

"You'll stop by tomorrow, won't you?" Skyler asked Jess, sounding a little desperate.

"Yeah. Sure. At noon?"

"That would be great." Her little sister plastered a big smile on her face. "Okay, kids. Say goodnight to your Auntie Jess."

Jess hugged the kids goodnight—Kaylie actually let her—and before she knew it, she was alone in the house with her parents.

"I think I'm going to bed," Thomas said, yawning. "We've been really busy this week. These old bones aren't used to working so hard." He grinned and hugged Jess. "I'm so glad you're home for Christmas."

"Me, too," Jess said, meaning it. She was happy to see everyone. She just wished she could get along with her mother.

"I'll help you clean up," Jess told Florence as they picked up mugs and plates. She followed her into the kitchen and began rinsing out the mugs and placing them into the dishwasher. Her mother remained silent as they worked.

"I'm glad you made sugar cookies," Jess offered. "You know they're my favorite."

"The grandkids really like them," Florence said.

Trying again, Jess said, "I should get the recipe from you. It was grandma's recipe, wasn't it?"

Florence turned and looked at her. "Why? Are you going to make them just for yourself?"

Jess shrugged. "Maybe. Or I might have kids someday and will want to make them." She struggled not to sound insulted.

"Hm. I suppose," Florence said as she wiped down the counter.

Jess gave up trying to talk.

"Well, I'm off to bed. Do you need anything?" Florence asked.

"I know where everything is," Jess said. She followed her mother into the living room where Florence unplugged the Christmas tree, then began turning off the lights.

"Goodnight."

"Goodnight," Jess said, watching her mother walk to the staircase.

Florence turned at the bottom of the stairs. "Aren't you coming up?"

Jess stared at the clock over the sofa. It was only ten. "I think I'll pick a book from the shelf down here and read a bit."

"Suit yourself," Florence said, then headed up the stairs.

The old house sat silent.

Most nights, Jess rarely returned home by ten, let alone went to bed that early. Her days were a whirlwind of appointments, court appearances, and endless meetings with couples, trying to coax them to agree on a settlement. Or to agree on anything at all. She ate lunch and dinner at her desk and drove home blurry-eyed and exhausted. Her life left little room to date, let alone maintain a relationship. The two times she'd tried to keep a relationship alive, the men had grown tired of her work hours. She didn't blame them. She was tired of her work hours too.

Jess wandered over to her grandmother's bookcase and studied the many titles. Both her Grandma June and her mother loved to read. Jess was certain her mother had a pile of books on her bedside table, just as her grandmother always had. They'd been so much alike, yet so different. It had always baffled Jess how her mother and grandmother could live in the same house in complete harmony when Florence couldn't seem to do the same with her own daughters.

Thinking of her Grandma June, Jess wondered why her parents still had their bedroom upstairs. The primary bedroom downstairs had belonged to her grandparents since Jess was born, but they were gone now. Her Grandpa Patrick died in 2017 after a long battle with cancer, then Grandma June passed in 2019 after a bout of pneumonia that lasted weeks. Jess didn't come home for Christmas that year and found it easier to keep making excuses each year after that. Without her grandmother to act as a buffer between her and her mother, Jess couldn't bear struggling through a family holiday.

Curious now, Jess padded down the hallway rug to the back of the house where her grandparents' room was. She turned on the light and sucked in a breath. The room was exactly as it had been when her grandmother was alive. The same wedding ring quilt covered the queen-size bed, and cream doilies still lay underneath the lamps on each nightstand. The dresser had been left untouched, with her grandmother's silver hairbrush and mirror that had been a gift from Patrick. Jess could still smell her grandmother's favorite perfume, White Linen by Estee Lauder, as she entered the room.

Jess walked to the dresser and picked up the hand mirror. It was heavy. The silver had been polished recently. In fact, the dresser was also dust-free. Her mother must clean this room regularly. Jess saw the bottle of White Linen and picked it up. She sprayed a tiny spritz on her wrist, then rubbed it into her other wrist. Jess smiled when she remembered the many times her Grandma June had done this for her as a child.

"Even little girls need to smell beautiful," Grandma June had said.

A small jewelry box also sat on her grandmother's dresser, and Jess lifted the lid and peered inside. There, on the burgundy velvet, lay her grandmother's pearl necklace, various pairs of earrings, and the gold wristwatch she wore daily. Jess frowned. Where was her grandmother's Christmas necklace?

Closing the lid, Jess turned out the light and left the room. She didn't want to snoop through her grandmother's belongings to find the necklace. Perhaps her mother had it in her room. Or maybe she'd given it to Skyler.

Jess had always loved the story of the Christmas star necklace when her Grandmother June told it each Christmas Eve. It was so sweet how her grandfather had saved his money to give her that one nice gift so she'd forever remember their first Christmas together. Jess had always hoped she'd find a man as kind and sweet as her grandfather had been. Now, she realized the likelihood of that was very slim.

No longer feeling like reading, Jess turned off the downstairs light and headed upstairs to her room. She still wasn't sleepy. Once in her room, Jess glanced around at her sister's trophies on the shelves over her bed, the corkboard with medals and ribbons pinned on it, and then the nearly empty shelves over her own bed. Elaina had been the athlete in the family, not Jess.

Walking over to her own shelves, Jess took down the old, dusty stuffed elephant Jay had won for her at the county fair.

She closed her eyes and tried to remember if she had been sixteen or seventeen. They'd been friends all their lives, but then one day, she'd watched him running during track practice after school and realized that she had stronger feelings for him than just as a friend. By the time they were sixteen, they were a couple, and by graduation, everyone thought they'd eventually marry. But that never happened. Instead, they went their separate ways.

Hugging the elephant, the bombardment of so many memories all in one day was too much for Jess. She slipped on the old coat she'd thrown on the bed earlier, pocketed a couple of items, then grabbed the throw blanket from the end of her bed and headed to the large dormer window. Jess opened it as she'd done a million times as a kid and teen and climbed out.

The window's ledge was wide enough to sit on and maintain your balance. The air was brisk, but there was no wind to sting her face. Jess wrapped the blanket around herself and gazed around the small town. Some stray Christmas lights were still on, as well as a few lights in neighbors' windows. A town like Redmond generally rolled up its streets by ten o'clock. Pulling a pack of herbal cigarettes from her coat pocket, Jess lit one and drew in a deep breath. Instantly, she felt calmer.

A loud bang came from below, and Jess craned her neck to see what it was. Probably a stray cat digging in someone's garbage. Then, a head suddenly appeared above the incline of the roof, making Jess jump.

"It's just me," a male voice said, then chuckled. The man stepped onto the roof and joined Jess on the window ledge.

"You scared me half to death," Jess said, glaring at Jay. "How on earth did you get up here?"

"The same way I got up here all those times years ago."

He laughed softly. "The old ladder was still lying beside my parents' house."

Jess couldn't help but smile. "You're lucky that wooden ladder didn't rot after all these years. Although it would have been funny watching you fall off it."

"Gee. Thanks."

"I'm just kidding. Why aren't you still working? Don't bars stay open until two?" Jess asked.

"Not my bar," Jay said. "I don't want wives coming after me for serving their husbands until all hours of the night. I know all these people."

Jess snorted. "You mean you went to school with all these people."

"You did too," he reminded her gently. Then he grimaced. "Are you smoking up here?"

Jess had moved her hand out of his view but decided that was silly. She was an adult, after all. "I don't smoke cigarettes anymore," she said. "It's herbal."

Jay's brows rose. "Herbal?"

Jess rolled her eyes. "Not cannabis, idiot. Herbal. Here." She handed him what was left of her cigarette.

Jay took a puff and started coughing. "That's got mint in it. It's awful!"

"Quiet," she admonished him. "Do you want to wake the neighborhood and get caught?"

He laughed again. "Boy, does this bring back memories."

Jess crushed out her cigarette in the glass votive holder she'd used as an ashtray as a teenager. "Yeah, nothing ever changes, right?"

"Apparently, you didn't get the memo that styles have changed. Did you buy that coat at a garage sale?" he asked.

Jess looked down at her junior high jacket. "Mom handed it to me as we headed out the door tonight. Can you believe she still has it?"

"Yes, I believe that. But the fact that you're wearing it is what I don't believe," Jay said.

"Maybe it'll come back in style," she teased.

A lone car drove by, drawing their attention to it. Jess changed the subject. "My coat isn't the only thing my mom's kept. I went into my grandparents' bedroom tonight, and it's as if they were still alive. Everything is right where my grandmother left it." She shivered. "Kind of weird, don't you think?"

Jay shrugged. "Not really. Your mother and grandmother were really close. It's probably hard for your mom to let her things go."

"Yeah, I guess. My room is still the same too. Elaina's things are on her side of the bedroom. It's kind of intimidating, knowing I'm still competing against my older sister even though she's been gone all these years."

Jay turned to look at her. "That's rough. It's like your mother wants to keep reminding you of that day."

"As if I could forget," Jess murmured.

"Maybe it's time you told her what happened," Jay suggested.

Jess slowly shook her head. "It doesn't matter how it happened. All that matters is the wrong daughter died that day, and I've been paying for it ever since."

Jay reached for her hand. "Hey. You don't really believe that, do you? Your mother would never have wished either of you dead."

Jess looked down at his hand holding hers, then slowly pulled hers away. "She may not have wished it, but it happened anyway, and her favorite died. Elaina was everyone's favorite—even mine."

Jay turned to look out over the town. "Yeah. Like you said. Nothing ever changes."

"What made you move back here? You'd escaped. I'd heard that you had a great job in Seattle and married a gorgeous woman." Jess glanced at his house next door. "Is she here with you?"

"No. We divorced a while back. She was way more ambitious than I was, and I couldn't keep up," Jay said. "But it was for the best."

"Sorry. So why come back here?"

"Because I no longer enjoyed my job. I didn't like working for a big corporation that knocked you down at every turn, and I wanted peace in my life again," Jay said. "My parents were selling the house so they could move to Florida, and I immediately decided I wanted it. I wanted to come back and be able to breathe again."

Jess thought about what he'd said. She couldn't blame him. She'd felt confined and trapped in her life at times too. But coming home had never occurred to her. It would be just as stressful.

"I get what you're saying. So, you bought the bar too?"

"I did. The sale of my house out there was sufficient enough to buy this house and the business. I remodeled both to make them my own, and it was the best decision I've ever made. I love working for myself and being around people who know me."

"Weren't you managing a department in a big advertising firm? How do you go from that to bartending?" Jess asked.

"Easily." Jay grinned. "I bartended in college, and I loved

it. The corporate world is all about who can talk the loudest and fastest about themselves. When you bartend, it's about the customer, not you. I like that."

Jess watched his face light up as he spoke, and it made her smile. They were twenty years older from when they'd first started dating, yet he still looked young and carefree. Well, not teenage young, but still handsome and appealing.

"What?" he asked, looking at her.

She hadn't realized how long she'd been staring at him. "Uh, nothing. I'm glad you're happy with your life, that's all."

"What about you? Are you happy with your life?" Jay asked, sounding genuinely interested.

"You found me sitting on a window ledge on a roof in the middle of the night, smoking. What do you think?" she joked.

He smiled. "Come on. I told you my story."

She sighed. "I do like my life, and sometimes I hate it. My job is demanding, but I'm good at it. I love my townhouse and the quiet little neighborhood, but the drive into Minneapolis every day is grueling. Do I like my life? I don't know. It's where I am right now."

"It's where you are right now? Where do you want to be?" Jay asked.

Jess shrugged. "I'm not sure."

"Are you involved with anyone?" Jay asked.

"No. Men don't like women who work all the time. What did you call it? Ambitious?" She watched for his reaction.

"Hm. Is that what you are? Ambitious? Or just overworked?"

Jess let out a long sigh. "I used to be ambitious. I thought if I succeeded, it would make up for Elaina dying. But it didn't. My parents don't care if I'm the best lawyer in Minnesota or the worst. They don't care how much money I make. Those things never impressed them. I don't know why I thought it would."

"I knew you the first eighteen years of your life. I don't believe that any of those things impressed you either," Jay said.

"Well, it's funny the things you can make yourself believe, isn't it?" Jess asked.

"Yeah."

They sat in silence for a long time, watching the moon rise higher, and the stars twinkle in the winter sky. Jess pulled the blanket closer around her.

"I'm bringing home a tree tomorrow night. Would you like to help decorate it?" Jay asked.

Jess brightened. "Maybe. That would be fun. What time?"

"Come over about eight. You should be able to sneak away from the family by then."

"It's a date," she said. Jess watched as Jay headed back down the roof and onto the ladder. It was as if all the years between high school and now had been swept away. She was still the mixed-up girl who'd lost her big sister—her best friend—and felt guilty as hell about it. All these years hadn't wiped those feelings away.

Heading back into her bedroom, she closed the window, pulled the shades, and went to bed.

CHAPTER FIVE

December 22, 2022

Jess awoke late the next morning and hoped everyone would be at work by the time she headed downstairs. She showered and dressed, then walked down the stairs. To her surprise, she heard sounds coming from the kitchen.

"So, you finally got up," Florence said as Jess entered the kitchen. "I didn't think you'd sleep so late."

"I'm usually up early and out the door to beat the traffic," Jess said. "It was nice sleeping in. You didn't have to wait for me. I can make my own breakfast."

"I wasn't waiting for you. I had some work to do before I go to the store today." Florence pulled a roast out of the refrigerator and placed it in a big roasting pan. Then she set peeled potatoes and carrots around it. "I thought I'd have everyone over for dinner tonight," her mother said. "Since you'll only be here for a few days, I know they'd all like to visit."

"That'll be nice," Jess said. She grabbed a mug from the cupboard and headed for the coffee machine. "I see you replaced Mr. Coffee with a Keurig."

Florence glanced her way. "Yeah. The kids kept bugging me to get one. It's easier to make one cup at a time."

Once she started the coffee, Jess pulled a skillet out from under the stove and headed to the fridge. She grabbed two eggs and broke them into the pan. Normally, Jess wasn't one to eat breakfast, but today it sounded good.

"I thought I heard voices coming from your room last night," Florence said.

Jess tried not to look as startled as she felt. "Oh. Really?" She kept her eyes on the eggs in the pan. "A friend of mine called to make sure I got here safe," she lied. "I must have had it on speaker."

"A friend?" Florence asked, brows raised

"Yeah. Just someone I work with," Jess said casually. For the life of her, she didn't know why she was lying. So what if Jay had been sitting on the ledge with her last night. Jess felt like she was still fifteen and had to lie. She changed the subject. "I noticed grandma's room still looks the same. I figured you and dad would take that room."

Florence continued preparing the roast and vegetables, then covered them and placed them in the refrigerator. Finally, she turned toward Jess. "There's no need for us to use that room. Our room upstairs is fine. If we get too old to use the stairs, maybe we'll move into it."

Jess nodded, not sure what else to say. She flipped her eggs, then took down a plate and set them on it after a couple of minutes. The silence in the room was deafening. She didn't know how to talk with her mother. In fact, she never knew what to say to her. Their relationship had become that uncomfortable.

"I'm heading in to work now," Florence said. "You're having lunch with Skyler later, aren't you?"

"Yeah. I thought I'd drop by early and look over the shop."

"Good. Skyler seems stressed lately. It could be because of the Christmas holidays, I don't know. She hasn't confided in me. Maybe she'll open up to you."

Jess frowned. Her mother sounded resentful that Skyler wouldn't tell her what was bothering her. It wasn't like any of them had ever opened up to their mother, as far as Jess knew. "Okay," was all she said.

"If your grandmother were still here, Skyler would probably tell her. She seemed to always be able to get you girls to talk," Florence added.

Jess stiffened. She couldn't tell if her mother was mad about their close relationship with their grandmother or sad that no one thought of her that way. "Grandma had a way about her," Jess finally said.

"She did. Dinner will be at six. I'll be home by five." Florence left the kitchen to put on her coat.

Jess stood in the doorway. "Is there anything you'd like me to do to help with dinner?"

"Nope. It's all taken care of. See you later." Florence rushed past her and out the back door as if she were as uncomfortable as Jess.

"Okay," Jess said softly as she returned to the kitchen to eat her breakfast.

After eating, Jess walked into the living room and over to the bay window. Looking outside, she saw no one on the street, no sign of life whatsoever. At home, there was traffic up and down the neighborhood streets at all hours, lights on in people's homes, and people walking dogs or parents and children playing in the snow. As she looked at the park across the way, there wasn't even a footprint in the fresh snow. It was perfectly smooth. If she hadn't known any better, Jess would believe she was living in a scene from an old-fashioned Christmas card.

Turning, she glared at the fake Christmas tree. It wasn't a bad-looking tree; it actually looked quite real. It was the kind that had a sprinkling of fake snow on it that looked nice. But it wasn't real, and it wasn't decorated with her grandmother's beautiful glass and mercury glass ornaments. She could not for the life of her understand why her mother wouldn't want to use the ornaments that they'd used for decades. It made no sense. Unable to look at the tree for another moment, she ran upstairs.

Later, Jess put on her nice coat—not the terrible color block one—and drove downtown. It was twenty degrees out, and the wind was blowing hard as it usually did in this flat farmland area. Sometimes during a heavy snow, the town had to close the roads in and out because of white-out conditions due to blowing snow. Jess hoped she didn't end up stranded here longer because of weather like that.

Downtown was basically three blocks long, with brick businesses on both sides of the street. Jess parked in front of a cute little antique shop and ran across the street to Skyler's store, aptly named "Skyler's Boutique." Her parents' hardware store was right next door. She stopped a moment and stared into the large glass window of the hardware store to look for her father. She remembered doing this as a child and even as a teenager. She'd press her nose against the glass to make her grandfather or father laugh. She finally caught sight of her dad grabbing something off a shelf and waved. He smiled and waved back.

The beautifully carved wooden sign that hung over the entryway to Skyler's business swung in the wind as Jess passed under it and entered. Immediately, she was immersed in a whole different world. Skyler had the eye and decor prowess of an interior decorator without the fancy education. Soft music played from above as the light scent of candles on display greeted her. The shop had old hardwood floors that Skyler had refinished, and plush rugs created separate areas throughout the space. There were little nooks created by cozy chairs, end tables, and bookcases, each displaying beautiful gift items. Local artwork hung strategically on the walls, and locally made pottery, stained glass, and woodwork were placed around the nooks.

"You made it," Skyler said, coming out of the backroom door behind the antique glass counter. Jess remembered how excited Skyler had been to save the counter that had once been a display area in the old drug store.

"Yeah," Jess responded. "The shop looks amazing. I could spend all day walking around in here."

Skyler grinned. "That's the point." She looked chic and professional with her long blond hair up in a twist and wearing a soft pink sweater dress. She was so tiny and petite that she could be one of Santa's elves.

"Is there anything in here that mom has admired?" Jess asked. "I came empty-handed for her. I had no idea what she'd like."

Skyler walked over to a 24x36 inch framed print of a loon on water carrying its baby on its back. It was stunning with the natural wood frame, deep blue water, and green reeds in the background. "Mom loves this picture. A local photographer took it. She said she'd hang it in the dining room."

"Where grandma's picture of the old farm is?" Jess asked.

"That's what mom said. I don't blame her. She hasn't

changed much in that house our whole lives except to update the living room furniture," Skyler said.

"And the Christmas tree," Jess murmured.

"You're really offended by that tree, aren't you?" Skyler teased.

Jess was, but she changed the subject. "Wrap up the picture, and I'll pay you after lunch. I agree with mom for once—that picture is much nicer than the old farm picture."

A tall, slender young girl with long red hair walked through the door and greeted Skyler.

"Hey," the girl said. "I came as quickly as I could. I had to wait for my brother to show up at the gas station, and he's always late." She put emphasis on the 'always.'

"No problem, Ardie," Skyler said. "This is my sister, Jess. I don't think you two have met."

"Hi," Jess said.

"Hi," Ardie said. "So, you're Skyler's big sister, the famous lawyer from Minneapolis."

Jess laughed. "I wouldn't say famous. I'm just a lawyer there. It's nice meeting you."

"Yeah. It's nice meeting you too." Ardie turned to Skyler. "Go enjoy your lunch. I can work until five if you need me."

"Great. We have a lot of things to wrap for customers," Skyler said. She walked into the back room with Ardie and returned with her coat on. "Okay. Let's go."

"Famous lawyer?" Jess asked under her breath as they walked out the door.

"I never called you that. But considering how few people actually leave this town, I'm sure she heard it from someone else," Skyler said.

Jess couldn't imagine anyone was talking about her in this

town, but then again, it was a small town. "So, where should we eat?"

"I don't know; there are so many choices," Skyler said, rolling her eyes. "There's a little sandwich place across the way. It's good. They're only open for breakfast and lunch. Let's go there."

"Sounds good." Jess followed her across the street.

People looked up from their lunches and smiled and waved as Jess and Skyler entered the small eating establishment. They found a booth in the back and looked over the menus that sat on the table.

"Hi, Skyler," the waitress said as she approached the table. "It's good to see you."

"Hi, Mindy," Skyler said. "I usually pick up my food, but today's special. My sister is with me."

Mindy smiled over at Jess, but nothing was said about her being the famous lawyer, thank goodness. "What can I get you ladies?" she asked.

They each ordered a half sandwich and soup and then were left alone.

"So, how's it going with you and mom?" Skyler asked with a wicked grin.

Jess rolled her eyes. "The same as usual. We keep trying to make small talk, but we're failing. It's like we're strangers. She knows nothing about my life and doesn't share anything about herself. It's weird."

"You should be used to it by now. You two have been doing this since—" Skyler stopped. "Sorry. I didn't mean to bring that up."

"Since Elaina died," Jess finished her sentence. "It's true. Mom's been blaming me for her death since that day, and there's nothing I can do about it."

"She doesn't blame you. All she's ever asked is for you to tell her what happened in the car that day," Skyler said.

"And I've told her repeatedly that it was just an accident and there was no blame on anyone. But she won't take that as an answer," Jess said, irritated. This was why she never came home anymore. Even after twenty years, it always came down to the day Elaina died.

"Is this why you asked me to lunch?" Jess asked.

Skyler shook her head. "No. I'm sorry. I never meant to talk about this."

Their food came, and they both turned their attention to it. After a few bites, Jess said, "I was in grandma's bedroom last night. I didn't see her Christmas star necklace in the jewelry box. Did mom give it to you?"

Her sister's brows furrowed. "No. I don't have it. Didn't mom tell you?"

"Tell me what?"

"We haven't seen the necklace since the Christmas before grandma died. Mom looked everywhere for it. It just vanished," Skyler said.

Jess frowned. "Why didn't anyone tell me?"

Skyler cleared her throat. "Well, mom wondered if you'd taken it after the funeral. She didn't accuse you of it, but she mentioned it to me one day."

"What? I never would have taken it. It was mom's to do with as she wanted. Why didn't she just ask me?" Jess was infuriated that her mother would think she'd take something that wasn't hers.

"Well, you and grandma got along so well, and mom just thought you wanted it to remember her by. She wasn't mad or anything. She just wanted to know where it was," Skyler said.

"I don't have it," Jess said louder than she'd meant to. She forced herself to calm down and said in a softer tone, "I wish you or her would have just come out and asked me. I hate that everything is so hush-hush all the time."

"I'm sorry. I figured mom would ask you."

They sat in silence again. The lunch crowd was thinning out, and the noise in the place quieted.

"Sorry," Jess said, fidgeting with her napkin. "I hate when mom assumes things."

"It's okay," Skyer said. She ate a few spoonfuls of her soup, then looked up at Jess. "Chris is cheating on me."

Her words startled Jess so much that she thought she'd heard wrong. "What?"

Skyler took a breath. "Chris is seeing someone else. Well, not someone; it's the secretary at his father's insurance business."

Her food forgotten, Jess leaned in. "Has someone told you that?"

Skyler shook her head. "I saw them."

Jess sat back against the booth, stunned. "When?"

"Six months ago. It was the end of June, and I was in a hurry to pick up the kids from daycare. I drove down the alley as a shortcut, and there they were, behind the office, kissing."

"Did Chris see you?" Jess asked.

"No. They were in the back door alcove. I guess he thought it was shaded enough so no one would recognize him. But I did. His suits are custom-made, and he buys expensive shoes. I'd recognize those shoes anywhere. They cost more than my entire wardrobe." Skyler was growing angry now. "He makes excuses all the time to be away from home. He says he's show-ing a house to someone or needs to work late at the office. I've followed him. He's seeing her instead."

"Oh, honey, I'm so sorry." Jess's heart went out to her sister. She'd never liked Chris, but she hadn't wanted this to happen to Skyler. "Have you told him you know?"

Tears filled Skyler's eyes. "No. I don't know what to do. He earns the majority of the money. We're in debt up to our ears with the lake house he couldn't live without, and I don't think I could support the kids with just my business. I feel stuck."

Jess felt her blood pressure rise. She wanted to punch Chris in the face. "There's a lot you can do," she said, putting on her divorce attorney hat. "If you sold the house, he'd have to give you half the equity. He'd also have to pay child support since he makes the larger income. I'm sure you could find a suitable place to live on your income, especially in this town. You don't have to put up with his cheating on you. You deserve better."

Skyler dropped her head and dabbed at her eyes with a napkin. "I shouldn't have said anything. I hadn't meant to. It just came out. I didn't want to put you in the middle of this."

"Hey. I'm your big sister. You can tell me anything. I want you to feel you can confide in me," Jess said gently.

Her sister raised her striking blue eyes that, until that moment, Jess hadn't realized looked so much like their mother's.

"I know you hate Chris. And now I've given you a good reason to hate him. I should have left you out of it," Skyler said.

Jess sighed. "Please don't drop this bomb on me and then close me out. I can help you. You're right; I'm no fan of your husband's, but I love you and the kids, and I want what's best for all of you."

"I have to think this over," Skyler said, shaking her head. "What if it's just a fling and he gets tired of her? Maybe he's feeling the same pressure I am over how much money we owe."

She looked into Jess's eyes. "Maybe it's just a distraction, and he still loves me."

Jess had heard all these excuses so many times before. Women coming to her for divorce advice and then talking themselves into staying. She'd watched women get the shaft so many times because they waited too long to act. The husband hid the money or spent it. She didn't want to see that happen to her sister.

"I can't tell you what to do, but at least do this one thing for yourself," Jess advised her. "Confront him. Get his story. See where he stands. Do it when the kids aren't around and in a non-confrontational way. Maybe he'll spill his guts and promise to never cheat again, or maybe he'll come clean. No matter what happens, you'll know better what you need to do."

"What if he chooses her?" Skyler asked, looking nervous.

"Do you really want to be with a man who doesn't want you?" Jess asked.

No longer hungry, they paid their bill and walked together to the shop. Before entering, Skyler pulled Jess aside. "Please don't say anything to mom or anyone else. I need to make up my mind first."

Jess nodded. "Client attorney privilege," she said jokingly, but her words fell flat. She hugged her sister. "You're worth so much more than you believe. Don't let anyone—especially Chris—tell you otherwise."

"Thanks, Jess. You know, I always felt like the outsider in the family because I was so much younger than you and Elaina. Now, I know how it must have felt for you two to be so close. And how hard it must have been for you to lose her," Skyler said.

Tears burned Jess's eyes. "You've never been an outsider.

You've always been my baby sister."

Skyler hugged her again and then headed inside the store. "I'll wrap up mom's gift and hide it in the store," she said, standing in the doorway. "She's going to guess it right away otherwise."

Jess nodded and then walked to her car. She'd been home less than twenty-four hours, and her life was getting more complicated by the second.

CHAPTER SIX

Christmas Eve 1965

June worked in the kitchen preparing Christmas Eve dinner as Flori sat in her highchair eating small pieces of a holiday sugar cookie. Pat had finally opened his hardware store in the corner building on November first with a little help from his father. Pat and June were surprised when his parents invested money into his store so he could finally realize his dream. They had also moved into the two-bedroom apartment above the store, which was part of the rental of the building. Not only was the apartment bigger than their other one, but they didn't have to pay extra to live there.

June moved a little slower tonight as she made gravy for their turkey dinner. Every few minutes, she stopped and leaned against the counter to take a few breaths. In the six years she and Pat had been married, she'd always made Christmas Eve dinner while he went to get a tree, and she wasn't going to change that now, despite how she felt.

"I'm home," a voice called from the living room. "Where are my favorite girls?"

June smiled to herself. "We're in here," she called out.

Pat came through the swinging kitchen door, but his happy expression quickly turned to concern. "You shouldn't be working like this," he said, hurrying to June's side and placing his arms around her. "I told you we didn't need to do anything special tonight."

Tears welled up in June's eyes. "But I wanted to. We've always celebrated Christmas Eve together."

Pat hugged his wife. "I know, Juni-bug. But the doctor said you shouldn't overdo it for a few days. I worry about you."

June's tears fell faster, and Pat led her to a chair at the kitchen table. He kneeled on the floor beside her, holding her hands. "Please don't cry, sweetie," Pat said. "We can still have a wonderful Christmas Eve."

"I feel terrible," June said between sobs. "I was really looking forward to another little baby in our future. I thought for sure this one would be different."

Pat held her hands tighter. "I'm sorry, Juni-bug. I'm as heartbroken as you that we lost the baby, but I'm thankful I have you and our sweet little Flori. I just want you to be healthy."

June nodded. "I know. We've been so blessed with Flori and now opening the store. And we have this nice, big apartment now too. Maybe I'm just asking for too much to want another baby."

Pat looked up into her eyes. "I'd love to have another baby, too. But maybe we should be careful for a year or two, just so you can get stronger. You've gone through a lot with the last two miscarriages. Give yourself a rest, sweetie. I don't want to lose you. I need you."

June knew he was right. She'd been pushing herself too

much between wanting to help him with the store and caring for Flori. She blamed herself for this last miscarriage—she'd been working too hard despite both the doctor and Pat telling her to rest.

"I'm sorry I didn't listen to you and slow down," she said, her words barely a whisper. "Maybe I wouldn't have miscarried if I'd rested like you'd told me to."

Pat grew serious and looked her straight in the eye. "Don't you dare blame yourself. You heard the doctor. He said it was too soon after your last miscarriage, and your body was too weak to keep the pregnancy. It wasn't your fault."

June squeezed her eyes shut. She'd been so emotional since coming home from the hospital, and it was hard not to blame herself. She knew Pat was right, but her heart was still broken.

"You're right. We should wait a while before trying again." She looked down at him as he sat there holding her hands. "I love you so much."

He smiled. "I love you too, Juni-bug." Pat stood and offered her his hand. "Now, you and Flori need to come into the living room and watch as I bring in the tree. It's tradition." He grinned, then lifted little Flori out of the highchair, spinning her in circles. The baby giggled with glee. Pat carried her to the living room and set her on June's lap on the sofa.

Pat opened the door and ran down the enclosed staircase. A few minutes later, he dragged up a big spruce tree, pulling it into the living room.

"It's beautiful!" June said, starting to get up to help.

"You just sit there, Juni-bug," Pat said. "I can put the stand on and set up the tree. You just relax."

Reluctantly, June sat and watched as her husband pulled the stand out of the box and adjusted the screws so he could place it over the tree trunk. Once it was on tight, he lifted the tree so it was standing upright.

"In front of the window?" he asked, looking over at June.

"Yes. Where everyone can see it from the street," June said. She looked down at Flori, who stared at the tree with wide eyes. "Wait until you see it with lights and ornaments," she told her little girl.

"Yep. She must think we're crazy, bringing a tree into the house," Pat said, chuckling.

Pat insisted on helping June get dinner on the table. He pulled the turkey out of the oven and placed it on the big ceramic platter that had once belonged to June's mother. He put Flori back in her highchair at their dining room table and then insisted June sit as he carried everything in.

"I'm not used to being waited on," June said.

"You should be used to it. If I could hire a maid for you to do all of this, I would," Pat said as he set the big turkey on the table.

"Then what would I do?" June asked, laughing. "You know I enjoy cooking and caring for Flori. I even enjoy helping in the store."

Pat sat down at the table. "But you deserve the best, Juni-bug. Someday, we'll buy a house and fill it with beautiful things. I want to give you everything you've ever wanted."

She reached over and took his hand. "All that sounds wonderful. But I have everything I want right here." June leaned over and Pat kissed her tenderly on the lips.

Flori squealed and laughed, making June and Pat laugh too. Pat carved the turkey, and they filled their plates.

"Are you wearing your Christmas charm?" Pat asked. "You know it's not Christmas unless you do."

June pulled the necklace out from under the collar of her dress. "It's right here."

Pat smiled. "There. Everything is as it should be."

June didn't think she could love Pat more than she did at that very moment.

Chapter Seven

2022

Jess was not in a good mood when she returned home. She was angry with Chris for cheating on her sister and upset with her mother for thinking she'd taken her grandmother's necklace. Why did her mother always believe the worst about her? Jess knew her mother blamed her for the car accident all those years ago. But then to think that she would take something of her grandmother's right after the funeral, well, that was just spiteful.

Jess walked over to the bookcase and lifted one of the old scrapbooks her grandmother had made decades ago. When she opened it, she saw the first date was 1959. Jess smiled. She knew these scrapbooks well. This one had her grandparents' wedding pictures, their first Christmas together, and other photos of her great-grandparents during the holidays. As she carefully turned each page, her heart warmed. Her grandfather had been a tall, handsome man when he was young and had looked good in his dark suit the day he married Grandma June. She wore a simple cream-colored dress with a full skirt that fell below her knees. They were married at the farm with only family members in attendance. Grandma June's father and brother were in the pictures too. Jess had never met any of her great-grandparents or her great-uncle because they had all died long before she'd been born.

She turned the pages, and there was a photo of her grandparents' first Christmas tree in the first apartment they'd lived in. Jess remembered her grandmother's stories of those years in the small place. They could have lived at Grandpa Pat's parents' farm, but Pat had been the one to insist they live in town. Grandma June had been a town girl her whole life, and he hadn't wanted her to feel isolated at the farm. Plus, it gave them the privacy they'd never have had at the farm.

So many of Grandma June's stories came to mind as Jess turned the pages of black and white photos. Grandma June had worked at the dime store until Florence was born, so she was able to buy things at a discounted price. That was why she could afford to own a Kodak Brownie box camera and develop the film. Jess remembered that camera. She and Elaina had used it to take pictures when they were little.

There were also photos of when her grandpa had opened the hardware store. He stood proudly behind the counter, wearing a green apron over his nice clothes. Jess knew it was green even though the photo wasn't colored because her father and brother wore green vests at the hardware store now instead of aprons. Jess was glad they had these old photos because they reminded her of her grandma's stories. But the stories had never been written down. Who would remember them once her mother and then she was gone?

A noise came from the kitchen. Jess heard someone opening the oven door and placing a pan in it. Her mother was home.

Setting down the photo album, Jess walked across the living room and through the kitchen door.

"Oh, hi," Florence said bluntly. She had pulled out a bowl from under the counter and was walking to the pantry. "How was your lunch with Skyler?"

"Interesting," Jess said, crossing her arms. "Can I help you with anything?"

"No. I'm fine. I was just going to cut up some apples and make an apple pie for dessert," Florence said.

"I can cut up the apples while you make the crust," Jess offered, walking toward the refrigerator. "The green ones, right?"

"You really don't have to do that," Florence said. "I can do both."

Jess sighed. It was just like her mother to block her out. "Then I can go set the table. How many are coming?" Jess opened the silverware drawer.

"You really don't have to do that," Florence said.

"Mom! I'm a grown woman. I think I can manage to set the table," Jess said, exasperated.

Florence tightened her jaw. "Fine. Set it for nine. But don't give the two kids knives. They only need a fork and spoon. And add a salad fork for everyone, too."

Jess started counting out the silverware. She had calmed down since this afternoon and didn't want to fight with her mom, so she said in an even tone. "Mom. I didn't take Grandma June's Christmas necklace. I just wanted you to know that."

Florence snapped her head up from where she was peeling apples. "I never said you did."

"Skyler said it was missing, and you thought I may have taken it after the funeral. I'd never do something like that. That necklace belongs to you."

"Skyler must not have heard me correctly," Florence said sharply, returning to peeling the apples. "I didn't accuse you of it."

"Either way, if you even thought I may have taken it, I didn't," Jess said. She grabbed the basket of napkins and headed for the kitchen door.

"I didn't say you took it," Florence insisted. "I just mentioned that you may have thought it belonged to you because you and mom were so close."

Jess turned back toward her mother, angry now. "That's the same thing as saying I took it. Why didn't you just ask me? I would have told you I don't have it. I hate how no one in this family ever just comes out and asks. Everything has to be so secretive."

"You're the last person who should be complaining about secrets," Florence said, staring hard at her.

Jess's shoulders sagged. "Don't start that again. Not now. There is no secret, Mom."

Florence stepped closer. Even though she was shorter than Jess, there was still that air of superiority that mothers managed to maintain over their children. "Then why don't you tell me what happened in the car that day? It's been twenty years. Yet you still won't say what happened."

"It was an accident," Jess said with more force than she'd intended. "Plain and simple. A stupid teenage accident that turned tragic."

"Something must have happened. You don't just run a stop sign for the fun of it. Elaina should have seen that truck coming a mile away in this flatland. She had to have been distracted. All I want to know is what distracted her," Florence said, raising her voice.

Jess's heart pounded. It always came down to this. "Wasn't it enough that Elaina died and I ended up in the hospital? What difference does it make?"

"Because there has to be more to the story," Florence insisted. "Just tell me!"

Jess shook her head. "It doesn't matter anymore. I keep saying that, but you won't listen." She turned toward the dining room. "I'm setting the table."

"You told your grandma, didn't you?" Florence asked, her tone accusatory. "But you won't tell me."

Jess turned back to her mother, her tone resigned. "I never told grandma. Or anyone else. Because it doesn't matter. Elaina's gone, and it won't make any difference." Jess left the kitchen, and thankfully, her mother didn't follow her.

Jess took a few deep breaths to calm down. How was she going to get through the next few days without going crazy? When Grandma June was alive, she'd ensure things stayed civil between Jess and her mother. But without her here, everything was wrong. Jess just wanted to get through the next few hours so she could escape the house and go to Jay's. At least there, she could be herself.

* * *

After what felt like a long, heavy silence, Jess's father came home, and then Rick and Mandy arrived with Skyler and the kids at their heels. But even though there was a crowd in the house, it didn't help to calm the tension.

"Where's Chris?" Jess asked Skyler quietly when she'd entered the house.

"Showing a house," Skyler said, her blue eyes flashing. "It's probably for the best. I think I'd blow up at him if he were here."

"Well, it wouldn't be the first fight of the day in this house," Jess said.

Skyler raised her blond brows, but Jess swiped her words away with the flick of her hand. "It's nothing. Just me and mom and the same old thing."

Skyler nodded. She knew what that meant.

Jess offered to help her mother in the kitchen and was promptly ignored. She went back into the living room, and Skyler went into the kitchen instead. Jess noticed her father watching her, but he never said a word. She knew he tried to avoid the fights between the girls and Florence.

Instead, Jess sat on the floor with Aaron and Kaylie and played with them. They had pulled out the large bucket of Legos and the old Playschool farm set, and Kaylie had taken a doll out of the closet too. Jess helped Aaron build a house with the Legos while playing with the farm animals with Kaylie. The kids made what had been a heavy day feel lighter. All they wanted was attention and someone to sit with them, and that's what Jess did.

Mandy and Skyler brought the food out and placed it on the table. Jess finally stood up and went to get the plates that she knew her mother would have warmed on the stove. Her mother ignored her, which was fine. Jess picked up the pile of plates and brought them out, setting one at each place.

Finally, they all sat down at the table and began filling their plates with food.

"I'm so happy we have all our kids and grandkids here," Thomas said, smiling at everyone. "Isn't this nice, Flori?" He turned to his wife.

"Of course, it's nice," she said, not looking up from filling her plate.

Jess knew that was her dad's way of trying to smooth things over, but it no longer worked that way. They weren't little kids who could be talked out of being upset at their mother anymore. At least she wasn't.

After a quiet beginning, chatter finally filled the room. Skyler urged Kaylie to eat while telling Aaron to sit down and stop fussing with his food. Mandy, who sat next to Aaron, was encouraging him to eat. Thomas and Rick talked about their day at the hardware store while Florence ate in dead silence. Jess was quiet too. She just wanted to get through this meal so she could leave the house—and the tension—behind for a few hours.

Florence brought out the fresh apple pie and whipped cream after everyone had eaten. The promise of pie had made the kids finally finish their dinner, and they sat there, wide-eyed, waiting for their servings. Skyler didn't have a piece, and Jess was too full to eat one too, but she accepted one just so her mother wouldn't take it personally. Finally, the meal was over, and they could move about helping to clear the table.

"Mom, why don't you relax and Jess and I can put everything away," Mandy suggested. She stood as if Florence had agreed and began carrying in a pile of plates.

Florence looked as if she'd protest but then nodded and went to sit in Grandma June's old wooden rocker. Jess quickly grabbed as much as she could from the table and headed into the kitchen. When the door closed, she sighed heavily.

"That bad, huh?" Mandy asked in a quiet voice.

"Yes. That bad," Jess said. "Thanks for offering to do the work. I can be away from her for a few minutes."

"Yeah, it's been pretty tense out there since we walked in. I figured something had happened between you and your mom," Mandy said.

Jess began scraping and rinsing the dishes. "We had a fight earlier."

"Well, if you need to talk, I'm here," Mandy offered. "First, though, I'd better clear that table."

Skyler joined them, and the three women put away the food and cleaned up the kitchen. They didn't say much because they all knew that if Florence heard them talking, she'd come in immediately to make sure they weren't talking about her.

"I'm sorry I can't stay long tonight," Skyler told Jess. "I'm sure you could use a buffer. But I need to get the kids home."

"I totally understand. I'll be fine. Mom and dad usually go to bed early anyway," Jess said.

As they finished cleaning up, Mandy told Jess, "Stop by the salon anytime if you want a break or to talk. We'll grab a cup of coffee and gab."

"Thanks, Mandy. I'll do that," Jess said. She felt lucky to have both Skyler and Mandy to talk to because she knew they both understood how difficult Florence could be.

Skyler rounded up the kids and left, then Mandy and Rick did also. As soon as they were out the door, Jess grabbed her old coat from the closet.

"I'm going for a walk," she told her parents as she headed to the front door.

Florence's head snapped up. "A walk? Tonight? Where on earth would you go?"

"I just want some fresh air," Jess said. "I'll be back in a while." She went out the door quickly before her mother could protest some more. "Sheesh. It's like I'm in high school again," she mumbled under her breath.

Jess walked to Jay's house and went up the driveway. She knocked on the kitchen door like she had a million times before years ago.

Jay was flushed, wearing a sweater with a blue buffalo plaid jacket over it. "Come on in. I just dragged the tree inside and I'm getting it into the stand," he said, smiling like a kid.

"I'll help." Jess slipped off her boots and jacket, leaving both in the kitchen. She followed Jay into the living room. "Wow. You've really changed this place," she said, glancing around. "I love it." The kitchen was now open to the living room with an island where the wall used to be. The big bay window in the living room had been replaced, and beams were on the ceiling, giving the living room a warm, country look. The house had been built in the early 1900s and had pretty much stayed the same for decades. But now, it looked warm and inviting.

"Thanks," Jay said. "I tore out the shag carpet, too, and refinished these beautiful hardwoods. I can't believe people covered them up."

"Trends change. Our kids will probably want shag carpeting," Jess said.

Jay winced. "I sure hope not."

He had a new tree stand in the living room in front of the bay window, so Jess helped him put it on the bottom of the tree, and then they both lifted it up. Jay crawled under it to adjust the tree.

Jess took in a deep breath. "I love that pine smell. That's what Christmas should smell like."

"That, and pumpkin pie and sugar cookies," Jay said.

Jess smiled. "Yes. Those things too."

Once the tree was standing straight, Jay started putting the lights on it. Since that was a one-person job, Jess wandered around the living room looking at pictures on the fireplace mantel. It was heartwarming looking at old memories beside the crackling fire. She picked up an old photo of Jay and her in their high school graduation gowns, smiling at the camera.

"I can't believe you still have this on the mantel," she said. "It was a hundred years ago."

"It was eighteen years ago," he corrected her, smiling. "And it was one of the happiest times of my life."

She turned and looked at him. "Really? Why?"

"Because I was still with you, and we hadn't gone our separate ways yet. That day I still believed you and I would be together forever," Jay said.

Jess set the photo down. "You knew I had a full academic scholarship to the University of Minnesota. I never said I'd follow you to Seattle."

Jay shrugged. "I know. But I had considered going with you until you broke up with me."

"You would have given up your track scholarship in Seattle to go to the U of M?" Jess was stunned. "That would have been crazy."

"Yeah. My parents said the same thing. But I wanted to go with you." He shrugged again. "It doesn't matter anymore. We went our separate ways."

She walked over and sat on the sofa. "And yet here we are again."

"Do you want something to drink?" Jay asked, changing the subject. "I think I have some Chardonnay in the fridge. Or maybe a bottle of red. Unless you'd prefer a good, boxed wine?" He grinned.

Jess laughed. "No boxed wine. We had enough of that in our teens."

"Hey. It was all we could afford," Jay said. He walked over to the kitchen, poured them a glass of Chardonnay, and then brought it back to her. "Merry Christmas," he said, touching her glass with his.

"Merry Christmas," she said softly, then took a drink. "Hopefully, I'll survive it."

Jay went back to putting lights on the tree. "Trouble at home?"

"Same old stuff. Mom won't let the day Elaina died go," Jess said. "I mean, I get that she will always miss Elaina because I do too. But why she thinks knowing what happened seconds before the semi-truck hit us will make a difference is beyond me."

"It might make a difference to her," Jay said gently.

"I don't know why," Jess said, shaking her head. "And did you know that Chris is cheating on Skyler? She saw him with his father's secretary, of all things. I always knew he was a creep."

Jay was quiet.

She looked up at him. "Did you know?"

He pushed his hair back with his hand and sighed. "I suspected he was cheating on Skyler. But it wasn't my place to say anything."

Jess frowned. "It certainly is your place to say something. Skyler is practically like a little sister to you. Did you see him with someone?"

"Owning a bar, I see all sorts of things. I try to mind my own business."

Even though it made her mad, Jess understood. "I suppose that's how you stay in business. You can't go running around telling spouses what you've seen in the bar."

"I'm sorry," Jay said. "I've only seen him having a drink with another woman occasionally in the evening. I never saw him act inappropriately. But I figured by the way they were flirting, something was happening."

"Poor Skyler," Jess said, shaking her head. "I told her I'd help her, but she's still in the phase where she thinks he'll come around and realize he needs her. I've seen it a million times. I hope Chris doesn't do anything stupid and leave her hanging without a house or money." She took another sip of wine. It felt good, warming her from the inside.

"Let's decorate the tree and forget about everyone else for a while," Jay suggested.

Jess agreed. She was already tired of the small-town drama.

Together, they placed Jay's family ornaments on the tree, along with a few cute Hallmark ones his mother had bought Jay and his older sister over the years.

"I can't believe your mom left these when they moved," Jess said, studying a mercury glass ornament shaped like Santa Claus. "They're so beautiful."

"She took a boxful of them but left the rest. She knew I'd never go out and buy any on my own," Jay said. "And she was right, as always." He grinned.

"Do they like Florida?" Jess asked. She'd always liked Jay's parents. His father had been a quiet man who worked as a heavy equipment mechanic, and his mother had been home full time. She was kind and listened without judging. Something Jess's mother wasn't able to do. There were many times Jess would come next door to rant after a fight with her mother. Mrs. Tannon would listen and try not to take sides. Jess had liked that.

"They like the warm weather," Jay said. "My mom is more

sociable than my dad, so she's joined some groups with other women. Dad likes to putter in the garage. And just like here, the minute he opens the garage door to work on something, the other men in the neighborhood come over to talk. It's kind of funny."

"I always liked your parents. I'm glad they're happy. How about your sister? How is she doing?" Jess hadn't known Jay's sister very well because she'd been five years older than them.

"Tamera is living in North Carolina on the coast and has two teenage children and a well-trained husband," Jay said, laughing. "They love it there, though. Mom and Dad are visiting them for Christmas this year."

"And you didn't want to go?" Jess asked.

"I went last year. This year, the bar was too busy, and I don't have as many workers as I did the first year. Covid hit this town hard."

Jess nodded. She remembered when her father told her he'd had to shut down the hardware store for a couple of weeks. "It spiked the divorce rate, though," she said. "We were our busiest a few months into Covid."

Jay stopped hanging ornaments and stared at Jess. "Really? I didn't know that."

"Yeah. Divorces were up around thirty percent higher, and it hasn't stopped. Newly married couples were hit the hardest, but even long-time couples came in. It put a strain on people having to spend that much time together."

"That's awful," Jay said. "Tragedies should bring couples together."

"They don't. They usually separate people," Jess said matter-of-factly. "It doesn't give me much hope about marriage."

"It must be hard, seeing that day after day," Jay said sympathetically. "I'm not sure I could stand it. Going through one divorce was enough. I'd hate to help people do that as my job."

"Someone has to do it," Jess said defensively. She started to hang another ornament when Jay reached over and placed his hand on her arm. It felt warm and comforting.

"I'm sorry. You're right. Someone has to do it. I hope you didn't think I was judging you," Jay said.

Jess looked up into his blue eyes and felt a tug at her heart. She liked the feel of his hand on her arm and the kind look on his face. He'd really grown into a handsome man—more so than the teenager he used to be.

"I know you weren't judging me," she said, pulling her arm away regretfully. "You don't judge people. You're nice like your parents. Your home still feels like a safe space."

He smiled. "Good. I want you to feel that way." Jay left and brought out the bottle of wine, pouring her another glass.

"Are you trying to get me drunk?" she asked, teasing.

His brows rose. "Maybe."

She laughed and took another sip of wine.

CHAPTER EIGHT

2022

Jess walked quietly into her parents' house, hoping not to wake them. She'd stayed at Jay's until midnight, much longer than she'd intended. After decorating the tree, they'd sat on the sofa with the lights off, enjoying the warmth of the fire and the twinkle of the Christmas tree lights. It had been so relaxing that she'd almost forgotten about the problems of the day.

Now, she just wanted to crawl into bed and start over tomorrow—hopefully, her mother wouldn't still be angry.

The tree lights were off, but Jess could still see the fake tree looming in the living room. She glared at it. After helping Jay decorate the fresh pine, she hated this tree even more. "Stupid fake tree," she said under her breath.

Jess crept to the staircase when suddenly she heard a noise in the kitchen. Jess stopped and listened. It sounded like someone was getting a plate and opening a drawer. She sighed. Probably her mother waiting up for her. Miffed that her mother was making her feel like she was still fifteen, Jess pushed through the kitchen door.

"Hi there, pumpkin," her father said, smiling up from his seat at the kitchen table. "Are you just getting home?"

All the anger left Jess. She saw her father had the pie dish out and was spooning a generous portion of whipped cream on a piece. "Were you waiting up for me?" she asked as she sat down across from him.

"Nope. I came down to sneak a piece of this delicious pie. Do you want some?" Thomas was already scooping up a piece for her.

Jess laughed. "Sure." She went to the cupboard, pulled down a plate, and then grabbed a fork. Her dad set a piece on the plate for her. Then he slid the bowl of homemade whipped cream over, and she spooned some on.

"Nothing better than your mother's apple pie," he said, savoring his first bite.

"No argument from me," Jess said. Her mother and grandmother both were good cooks and bakers. Something Jess hadn't inherited.

"Did you have a good time at Jay's house?" Thomas asked.

Jess stared at her father, surprised. "How'd you know I went to Jay's?"

He chuckled. "Where else would you go so late at night without your car?"

"I suppose," she said, taking another bite. "But don't tell anyone, okay? I don't want rumors flying around town. We just decorated his tree and talked. Nothing tawdry."

"That's what I figured," he said. He ate another bite. "Did you and your mother get into a row before we all came home?"

She grinned. "Wasn't it obvious?"

"Very obvious," he said. "When I walked into the house, it felt like you could cut the tension in the room with a chain saw."

Jess laughed. "Yeah. Nothing has changed. That's why I haven't been home in so long."

"I guessed that, too," Thomas said. "But you and your mother can't keep doing this dance forever. At some point, one of you will have to give in."

Jess shook her head. "That's the problem, Dad. Everyone always gives in to mom so she won't be angry. Grandma always gave mom her way, and you do too. I'm tired of having to appease her."

Thomas ate his last bite of pie, then carefully set his fork on the plate. "Your mother can be difficult, that's for sure. And I know she was sometimes tough on you kids, always trying to make you do better. But your mother always meant well. She knew life could be hard, and she wanted to make sure you kids could handle it."

"Sometimes she expects too much," Jess said. "We're all only human."

"That's true. But she never expects more from anyone than she does of herself."

Jess looked at her father quizzically.

"See that bowl of whipped cream?" Thomas asked. "Most people today do it the easy way and buy the can you can spray whipped cream from. Not your mother. She buys the cream and whips it up herself, just like her mother did. And that apple pie." He chuckled. "Well, what's left of it. Your mother could buy canned apple filling and put it in an already made crust, but she doesn't. She peels the apples herself and makes the crust from scratch. When your mother does something, she does it the right way, even if it's harder. She never chooses the easy way out."

"Are you saying I choose the easy way out?" Jess asked,

feeling offended.

"Not at all," Thomas said. "You're as hard a worker as your mother. Look at you. You went to school all those years to become a lawyer, and you've stuck with it and have worked hard. No, I'm not saying you're lazy in any way. I'm just saying that your mother doesn't expect more out of you or anyone else than she does of herself. And I have a feeling the reason you two butt heads is because you're more alike than different."

Jess's brows rose. "You think I'm like mom?"

Her father chuckled. "You are your own person, of course. But you both are strong women with strong characters. That's not a bad thing." He stood, took his plate to the sink, and rinsed it. Then he turned back to Jess. "Just think about that before judging your mom too harshly. Or judging those of us who just like to keep the peace." He gave her a kiss on the head and headed out the door. "Goodnight, sweetie."

"Goodnight," Jess said, feeling blindsided by his words.

* * *

It took Jess a while to finally get to sleep despite feeling exhausted from her stressful day. Her dad's words kept rolling around in her head, along with memories of her childhood. Her mother hadn't been mean, but you always knew when you'd disappointed her. She'd known how to use that to make you do the right thing. As a child, Jess had followed Elaina's lead of being the good girl who did everything her mother wanted. But as they'd grown into teens, they'd both realized that their mom didn't always know best. They had personalities of their own and wanted to go their own way. But instead of slowly giving the girls their freedom as they grew, Florence continued to tighten the reins.

Elaina had been the perfect daughter who did everything right, but she also had a wild streak and was a free spirit. She'd wanted to try new things and explore the world around her. So, when she chose to go to Berkely in California—and had earned a scholarship there—she couldn't have been happier. Elaina wanted to go far away to school and get out from under the mother's thumb. But Florence was completely against it. She'd wanted her favorite daughter close. That was the fight they'd been having in the kitchen the day of the accident.

Jess had always known Elaina was her mother's favorite, and it had never bothered her. That was because she knew she was her grandmother's favorite, and somehow that peeved her mother, which was an added bonus. Even after Elaina died, Jess never achieved favorite status with her mother. In fact, because of the accident, they'd grown even further apart.

Finally, brushing away the thoughts of the past, Jess fell into a fitful sleep.

* * *

The next morning, Jess awoke even later than the day before. This time, much to her relief, no one was home when she went downstairs. It was the twenty-third of December, with Christmas Eve only a day away. And still, three more days until she could leave. It felt like an eternity.

Jess made herself breakfast and then called Skyler to see how she was doing.

"Hi, little sister," Jess said, trying to sound more upbeat than she felt. "How are you this morning?"

"Hi," Skyler said, sounding tired. "I had a bad night. After

I put the kids to bed last night, Chris came home, and we had a big fight."

Jess grimaced. "How did that go?"

"Not well. I should have stayed calm and done what you said. I should have talked to him when we weren't angry. Instead, I accused him of cheating, and of course, he lied and said I was delusional. When I told him I'd seen him kissing his father's secretary in the alley, he was surprised but came up with a story about that, too. He said he was just reaching across her, unlocking the door, and I had seen nothing." Skyler sighed. "I know what I saw."

"Trust your instincts," Jess said firmly. "Don't let him bully you. If you believe he's cheating on you, then more than likely, he is."

"It gets worse. He told me I was crazy, then threw some of his stuff in a bag and stormed out. He was gone all night. I know he was with her."

"Oh, Skyler. I'm so sorry. Have you seen him yet today?"

"He came by the shop this morning, and the fight started again in the back room. I asked him where he'd slept last night, and he said at the hotel in town. But that was a lie. I'd called there last night and asked if he was registered. When I accused him of being with her again, he went berserk. He said I'd better get my shit together for the kids and that he could find someone less crazy than me. It was terrible.

"What am I going to do, Jess?" Skyler said, sobbing. "I can't afford to leave him, and I can't keep living this way. All I do is worry about where he is and who he's with. I don't want to take the kids from him, but they can't have a mother who's obsessive, either. I feel like I'm stuck."

"Do you want me to come to the shop so we can talk?" Jess

asked, already leaving the kitchen to get her coat.

"No, no," Skyler said. "It's really busy today, and I need to get ahold of myself. I'll call you later, okay?"

"Okay," Jess said. She felt terrible for Skyler and wished there was something she could do for her. Feeling restless, Jess ran upstairs to get her warm coat and put on her boots. Then she headed to her car to drive downtown.

Jess wasn't sure where she should go; she just knew she didn't want to be in the house. She also decided she'd check on Skyler at lunchtime, and maybe they could talk. After driving up and down the street, she decided to stop in at Mandy's hair salon.

Mandy's salon was on the same block as the hardware store and Skyler's boutique. In fact, both Skyler and Mandy rented from her parents, who owned the entire block. Jess's grandparents had started the hardware store and eventually bought the building, then began to invest in the attached buildings as well. Her parents added on when they took over the hardware store. It was quite convenient for Skyler and Mandy.

Parking in front of Mandy's salon, Jess got out of the car and headed inside.

"May I help you?" A petite dark-haired girl sat behind the desk in the entrance.

"Hi. I was looking for Mandy," Jess said.

"Do you have an appointment?" the girl asked.

"Oh, she doesn't need an appointment, Sunny," Mandy said, coming over to the desk. "She's family." Mandy turned to Jess. "Come to the back room. I have some time before my next appointment."

The two women walked past four styling stations where three women and one man were busy cutting and styling hair.

Jess hadn't been there in a while, and it looked like Mandy had done some updates.

"The place looks great," Jess told her when they entered the back room. "You have a busy shop."

"Thanks. It's only crazy today because everyone wants to look good for Christmas. Lots of family rivalries," Mandy added with a grin.

"Boy, don't I know it," Jess said.

"Want some coffee? Or a Coke?" Mandy asked. They'd gone past a table with a coffee machine on it and into a smaller space with a desk Mandy used as an office.

"No, I'm fine," Jess said. "I just wanted to come by and see you."

"I'm glad you did. Go ahead and sit." Mandy pointed to a padded chair beside her desk and sat in her swivel chair. "So, you survived last night?"

Jess laughed. "Yes. After everyone left, I went over to Jay's and helped him decorate his tree. It was a relief to get out of the house."

"Yeah. Florence can be difficult sometimes. But it's only because she wants the best for everyone," Mandy said.

"You always see the good in people," Jess said, smiling over at Mandy. She noticed the dark circles under her sister-in-law's eyes. "Hey? Are you working too hard? You look tired."

"Tired? Or old?" Mandy joked.

"No. Not old. Are you feeling okay?"

"Well, just between you and me, we've started the process for IVF again," Mandy said. "The hormones are really getting to me. But it'll be worth it if we get pregnant this time."

Jess felt terrible that she'd been so obsessed over her own problems with her mother that she hadn't asked Mandy how she was. "I'm so sorry I've been complaining when you've had your own stuff going on. I had no idea you'd started again. I wasn't sure if you two would try again after the last two times didn't work."

"That's why I don't want anyone else to know," Mandy said. "If it doesn't take this time, it's better if the rest of the family doesn't know. It's even more depressing when everyone knows you've failed."

Jess leaned in closer to Mandy. "I can understand you wanting to keep it to yourself, but please don't think of it as a failure. You're trying, and that's what's important."

Mandy sighed. "I know. It's hard, though. It's so expensive, and then we get our hopes up. Rick would make such a great father. I feel like I'm keeping him from being one."

Jess's heart went out to Mandy. She was placing the blame on herself when she knew that neither of them were at fault. "Rick adores you whether or not you two have children."

Mandy smiled. "I know. And he says he's fine either way. We've also started the adoption process, just in case this doesn't work. I'm all for adopting a child, but I just wanted to try having a baby one more time. We've even talked about adopting a child even if the IVF works."

"That's great," Jess said. "No matter what you two do, you'll be great parents. I hope it works out for you this time."

"Thanks. I didn't mean to drop all of this on you. Please don't tell Skyler or Florence. They only get disappointed when it doesn't work."

"I won't," Jess said. "I doubt I'll be talking to my mother at all over the next few days." She laughed.

"I wish you two could smooth things over," Mandy said sincerely. "I know the problems go way back, but I hate to see you two butting heads all the time. I love both of you."

"I'm really trying," Jess said. "But I can't give my mother what she wants, and she won't stop until I do. It's an endless circle."

Mandy nodded. "Family is hard."

"Yes. Family is hard," Jess agreed.

"Speaking of which, is everything okay with Skyler? Her shop's back room shares a wall with my office here, and I heard her yelling at someone today. I think she was yelling at Chris, but the words were muffled."

Jess sighed. "They're having problems. Another secret we have to keep from my parents."

"I hope they'll be okay," Mandy said, looking concerned.

Jess shook her head. "I don't know. There's no easy solution."

Mandy stared out the door toward her salon. "Nothing is ever as it appears, is it? Everyone walks around saying they're fine, when the truth is, we're all dealing with something."

Jess nodded. Mandy had hit the nail right on the head. Jess just wasn't sure if her being home for Christmas was helping anyone's situation, least of all her own.

CHAPTER NINE

Christmas Eve 1968

June pulled the boxes of Christmas lights and ornaments out of the storage closet and carried them to the living room. Four-year-old Flori tried to help, but the boxes were too heavy. So, June handed her the small box that held the tree topper that she'd bought the second year they were married. Flori looked so cute as she walked purposefully across the apartment toward the front window where they would place the tree. Her dark hair had thickened from the fine baby hair she'd once had and hung nearly to her shoulders. Her bright blue eyes sparkled with delight in anticipation of her father bringing home their tree. June had dressed her in a brand-new red velvet dress with a full skirt that went to her knees. With it, she wore white socks with lacey edges and black Mary Janes. The dress had been expensive for their tight budget, but the moment June saw it, she had to have it for her little girl. Flori would only be little once, and since it seemed they'd never have another baby, June couldn't help but splurge on her.

Nervously, June reached up to her neck where her star

necklace usually hung. It wasn't there, a reminder of what she'd done to ensure Flori had a nice Christmas this year. The past three years since opening the hardware store had been tough on their budget. Even with the apartment being part of the rent, they'd struggled to buy their basic needs as Patrick tried to grow his business. June didn't begrudge Pat his dream—she believed in him and knew some day all their sacrifices would be worth it. But now that Flori was older, June wanted her to have a memorable Christmas. And if June had to sacrifice something to give her that, then so be it.

But she was nervous that Pat would notice the necklace was gone.

June was in the kitchen cooking dinner when Pat came home. Flori was pretending to cook, too, on the little play stove her grandparents had given her for her birthday. She had pots and pans and cooking spoons just like her mother and loved to mimic what June was doing.

"I'm home!" Pat called out when he came in the door. Flori dropped her spoon and ran out the kitchen door and into her father's arms. As June watched from the doorway, Pat swung his daughter in circles through the air. "Who is this little princess I see?" he asked after setting her down. "What a lovely dress you're wearing."

Flori looked down at her dress and smoothed it with her hands the same way June did. "Mommy bought it for me. It's pretty," Flori said in her little girl's voice.

Pat looked up at June and winked. "Mommy has good taste," he said.

"Did you bring the tree?" Flori asked, quickly forgetting the dress.

"Tree? What tree?" he teased.

Flori looked at him quizzically. "The Chismass tree," she said.

Pat chuckled at the cute way she said Christmas. "Well, let me look." He went out the door and down the stairs. Flori ran to the door to watch and giggled with glee as she watched him pull the big spruce up the stairs. She backed up when he came through the door, the tree dropping needles as it pushed through the door jam.

June smiled at the excited look on Flori's face. She went to help Pat put the stand on, then he lifted the tree and set it down on the floor. The tree branches fell into place.

That evening, after the little family ate their turkey dinner and stuffed themselves with the apple pie June had baked, they circled the tree placing ornaments on it. Little Flori put ornaments all in the same spot, making the tree look a little lopsided, but June didn't care. June and Pat placed them up higher and around the tree to balance it out. The only thing that mattered was they were celebrating as a family.

After tucking Flori into bed with promises that Santa Claus would leave her a surprise under the tree if she went right to sleep, the little girl did finally fall into a deep slumber. June quietly pulled out the gifts she'd wrapped for Flori and placed them under the tree. She had five in all, with one very large package overtaking the space. Then June hung the stocking that she'd stuffed earlier with small toys and candy up beside the tree. For Flori, this was going to be a memorable Christmas.

"That's a lot of gifts," Pat said as June joined him on the sofa. "I hope you bought them for cost through our store."

June nodded. "I did. Except for one because it wasn't available to order. I bought it at the dime store."

Pat nodded. Generally, he never questioned how June spent

money because he trusted she was being as careful as he was. Tonight, though, his question had made June's nerves tighten. She hoped he wouldn't ask her where the money had come from.

"I have a little gift for you," he said, surprising her.

"I thought we agreed not to spend money on each other." June hadn't bought him a gift this year. It had already been a stretch buying Flori's gifts.

"We did," Pat said. "But this is a special gift." He went to his coat and pulled a small box out of the pocket. Returning to the sofa, he handed the wrapped box to June.

She stared at the box, hoping he hadn't spent too much. "You really shouldn't have," she said.

"Open it," Pat said, giving her a small smile.

June carefully pulled off the red paper. It was definitely a jewelry box. Her heart began to pound. He'd spent too much, and she felt doubly guilty for what she'd done with her necklace. Lifting the lid, her eyes widened. Inside lay her beautiful Christmas star necklace.

"How?" she asked, raising her eyes to his.

"Jack brought it to me yesterday. He said he felt bad that you'd pawned it and wanted me to give it back to you. He told me you could keep the necklace while you make payments on it," Pat said.

June's heart clenched as tears filled her eyes. She'd hoped to be able to buy back the necklace before Pat learned she'd pawned it.

Pat tipped his head to look into her eyes. "Why, Juni-bug? Why would you pawn your favorite necklace?"

His words broke her heart. She felt so terrible for what she'd done. "I'm so sorry," she said, sobbing. "I wanted to give

Flori a memorable Christmas. Money has been tight, and I thought I could buy back my necklace before you found out. It was a stupid thing to do." She pulled a handkerchief from her pocket and wiped at her tears, but they continued to fall. June was so ashamed that she'd pawned her special necklace just to buy gifts.

"Ah, Juni-bug. Please don't cry." Pat moved closer and wrapped his arms around her. "I'm not mad. I was just surprised you'd done it. But you did it for a good reason, so how could I be angry?"

"But it's my special necklace. I treasure it, I really do. I was desperate to give Flori a nice Christmas," June said. "And all I've managed to do is hurt you."

"No, sweetie. You haven't hurt me," Pat said. "I was surprised at first. And then I realized how tough things have been for you. We both have worked so hard these past three years to make a success of the store, and we've pinched every penny to keep afloat. But it's not fair to you or to Flori. It's my fault, sweetie. I'm so sorry I've been thinking only of the store and not enough about you two."

June blinked away tears, completely stunned by what Pat was saying. "I don't feel like I've done without at all. I know you're trying to build a good life for Flori and me. And I don't mind working in the store or doing the books. We're a team, and I want us to be partners in this."

Pat smiled. "I want that too. I'll pay Jack back for what we owe on the necklace. And next year, we'll do our best to loosen the purse strings a little so we can give Flori a nice Christmas. I want you and our little girl to have only the best."

June hugged him close. "Thank you for understanding. I felt so awful, pawning my necklace. I promise I won't do it again."

Pat smiled as he pulled away. "Here," he said, lifting the box from her lap. "Let me put your necklace on for you."

June turned around and lifted her hair so he could clasp the necklace. When she turned back, he was still smiling at her.

"There," he said warmly. "Now everything is as it should be."

June's heart warmed as they snuggled together on the sofa, enjoying their Christmas Eve as the lights on the tree twinkled.

CHAPTER TEN

December 23, 2022

Jess wasn't sure what to do with herself after leaving Mandy's salon, so she drove around town for a while. She didn't want to bother Skyler yet, and she definitely didn't want to go home in case her mother was there for lunch. Finally, after circling the small town several times, she found herself pulling into the parking lot of The Pier.

The place was quiet when Jess walked in. She glanced around, wondering if she should sit at a table or the bar. Once she caught sight of Jay standing behind the bar smiling at her, she walked in his direction.

"Hi." He walked over to the side of the bar where Jess had sat down. "What brings you in here?"

She grinned. "If I said you, would you be flattered?"

"Extremely flattered, but I'm not buying it. What can I get you?" He reached under the bar and handed her a menu.

"Is it too early for a rum and Coke?" Jess sighed. She watched as Jay glanced toward the wall clock.

"Well, for some people in this town, no. But for you? I

think eleven-thirty is a bit early."

"Okay. Just make it a Coke, then." Jess opened the menu and stared at the contents. She wasn't very hungry, but it was almost lunchtime.

Jay placed the glass of Coke on the bar in front of her. "So, tell me what's wrong. You look stressed."

Jess took a sip of her Coke. "I am stressed. Between Skyler, my mom, and, well, other family issues, I'm going insane. I shouldn't have come home this year. Or any year, for that matter. Trouble seems to follow me."

Jay leaned on his side of the bar. "I'm glad you came home," he said, his voice low and deep. "Ignore everyone else, and come have Christmas with me." He winked.

She studied him for a moment, wondering if he was teasing or flirting. He looked good. Really good. She even liked his shaggy hair and the beginning of a beard on his face. She knew many guys worked hard for that look, but not Jay. This was just him. "Oh, if only it were that easy," she replied.

"Maybe it is," he said, standing up straight again.

The door opened, and light filtered in as people entered the bar. Jay went to wait on a couple of tables, leaving Jess to think about what he'd said. It would be so easy to fall back into a relationship with Jay. She knew him. They had history. But it had been a long time ago, and they'd both changed so much. Would it be the same if they were together now?

"What can I get you?" Jay asked, startling her out of her thoughts.

"Just a plate of fries," she said. "I'll stuff myself with carbs and wallow in self-pity."

He smiled. "Sounds like a plan."

Jess sat at the bar watching as the locals came in for

lunch. She watched Jay work effortlessly, talking to customers, pouring drinks, and taking orders. People liked Jay. He had an easy-going temperament that helped him get along with just about anyone. But he was also organized and efficient in his work. She couldn't help but think that he was right—this business was perfect for him.

"Here are your fries," he said, setting the plate down in front of her. "Wallow away."

She chuckled softly and did just that. The fries tasted good. Hot, crispy, and fattening. The perfect combination. Jess generally didn't eat junk food because she sat all day and rarely exercised. She tried to stick to salads, healthy wraps, and low-carb foods. The older she got, the harder it was to keep her weight down, and foods like fries didn't help. But today, they hit the spot.

"Feeling better?" Jay asked, stopping to top off her Coke.

"Yes. These fries are perfect. The waiter isn't bad either." She smiled.

"Well, I hate to ruin your carb buzz, but guess who just came in with a woman other than his wife?" Jay asked. He nodded to the right, and Jess turned to look. There sat Chris and a slender redhead in a booth near the back of the bar. They were leaning across the table, so close their faces practically touched.

Jess slid off the stool. "Mind if I punch him?" she asked Jay.

"I don't mind, but the sheriff is two tables over, and you might get arrested," Jay said.

Jess took a deep breath and stood up straight. She walked purposefully toward the table and stopped right next to it. Chris and the woman looked up, expecting to see the waitress. Their faces stopped smiling when they saw Jess.

"Well, well. Are you having a nice lunch?" Jess asked, glaring at Chris.

"Just walk away," Chris growled. "I have nothing to say to you."

"It sounded like you had plenty to say to your WIFE this morning," Jess said, turning to the woman. "You do know he's married, right? It would be a hard thing to hide in a town this small."

The woman had the decency to look embarrassed. Jess gave her credit for that.

Chris stood, staring down at Jess. "Whatever is going on is none of your business," he growled. "You're the one putting stupid ideas into Skyler's head. You bring trouble wherever you go."

Jess's heart began to pound. She clenched her fists. "As your wife's divorce attorney, I have every right to talk to my sister. Maybe you'd better go talk to someone, too."

Chris took another menacing step toward Jess, but she stood her ground. The bar had quieted down, and heads were turning to catch the show. Jay appeared and stood beside Jess.

"I think you and your friend should eat somewhere else," Jay told Chris in a tone that left little room for argument.

Chris glared at Jay. "Fine. We'd rather not eat in this greasy spoon anyway." He pushed past Jay, then turned back to Jess. "Keep your nose out of my family, or you'll regret it."

Jess laughed. "Too late."

Chris turned and walked out with his little chippie.

"Well, that was fun," Jay whispered to Jess as he led her back to her seat at the bar. "Now the whole town knows Skyler's business."

Jess's heart dropped as she realized what she'd done. "Crap.

You're right. I shouldn't have done that. But he makes me so mad!"

"I get it," Jay said. "I really do. But it'll be the talk of the town in less than an hour."

"I've got to go see Skyler," Jess said, standing up. She pulled her wallet out of her purse.

Jay raised a hand. "Don't worry about the bill. Go help your sister."

"Thanks," Jess said. "I mean it. Thanks for everything you've done for me the past couple of days."

He smiled. "I'm here for you, Jess. Always have been."

They stared at each other a moment, and everything Jess had felt for him eighteen years ago came rushing back to her. "Thanks," she said again softly. Then she hurried out of The Pier, feeling a dozen pairs of eyes on her back.

* * *

Jess walked into Skyler's boutique just as her sister was ringing up a sale for a customer. Ardie was there too, helping a woman across the shop. As Jess watched her sister, she noticed how tired she looked. Skyler always looked perfect, from her hair to her makeup and clothes. But today, she looked like she'd been crying all morning and didn't give a damn about her looks.

Once the woman walked away from the register, Jess went behind the counter and wrapped Skyler in a hug. "How are you doing?"

Skyler hugged her back, then pulled away. "Don't be so nice to me. I'll start crying again."

"Well, you may start crying once I tell you what happened. Can we talk in back?"

Skyler nodded, and they walked into the back room and into the small office space. "What happened?"

"I saw Chris at The Pier a few minutes ago. He wasn't alone."

Skyler sat down hard on her desk chair. "So, he's flaunting her all over town now."

"It looks like it," Jess said, grabbing a folding chair and sitting down too. "But I may have made things worse. I confronted him, and kind of became the center of attention."

"People already know he's taking this woman out around town. I'm sure other people have noticed, they're just too nice to tell me," Skyler said.

"What can I do to help?" Jess felt so bad for her sister. Skyler's life was falling apart right before Christmas in front of the whole town. It wasn't easy to keep those things quiet around here.

Skyler suddenly sat up straighter, her expression determined. "I'm done crying over him. He's not worth it. Tell me what I should do. I want him out of my life."

Jess nodded. "Okay. If you're sure. Get a locksmith to the house immediately before Chris gets there first. Change all the locks so he can't get inside. Be civil—don't toss his stuff out on the lawn and light it on fire. Believe me, some women have done that. Put his stuff in a suitcase and leave it on the porch. Whatever you do, don't let him in the house until a settlement is in motion."

"Okay," Skyler said. "That's what I'll do."

"We can formalize the separation after Christmas," Jess said. "By then, you'll know for sure if you want to leave him or try couples counseling."

Her sister shook her head. "No. This has gone on long

enough. I'm through." She bit her lip. "I'll be okay, right? I mean, if it gets really bad, I can move in with mom and dad, but I should be okay."

Jess's heart went out to her. It was going to be a long, hard road for her sister, and breaking up during the holidays made it all the more terrible. She pulled her into a hug again. "You'll be fine. Once all is said and done, I'm sure you'll be able to find a smaller house and support the kids. I'll be with you the entire time, I promise."

"Okay. I'll get the locks changed today."

Jess stayed with her a while longer to make sure she was fine. Once she got back into her car, she sat there, wondering where to go. She was positive her mother would be home. Well, she had to face her eventually. Sighing, Jess turned her car toward home.

Jess was surprised to find the house empty when she walked inside. She grabbed a bottle of water from the fridge and went upstairs to her bedroom. Sitting on Elaina's twin bed, Jess pulled her laptop from its case and opened it. She could start working on the paperwork for her sister's separation.

After working for a few minutes, she stopped and gazed around her. Jess couldn't believe she was working on her baby sister's divorce. Why did everything have to fall apart? She wondered what her grandmother would say about all this if she were still alive. Grandma June and Grandpa Pat had been in love until the day they both died. Her grandmother probably couldn't even fathom a marriage dissolving. Not that their life had been easy. Jess knew that her grandparents had suffered several miscarriages before deciding not to try having any more children. They had worked hard to build up the hardware store, and they had bought this Victorian house that had been left to rot and completely remodeled it. They'd been hard workers who believed in building things. What would Grandma June think of Jess now working to dissolve Skyler's marriage?

As Jess gazed around the room, her eyes fell on Elaina's senior picture. Elaina had been her best friend and confidant. After the accident, Jess no longer had anyone to tell her secrets to. Images of that last day, as they drove out of town in Elaina's yellow Ford Mustang, filled Jess's thoughts.

"I can't wait to get out of this town," Elaina said. Her window was wide open, and her long blond hair was floating all around her.

"I'll miss you, though," Jess told her. "It'll just be me and the younger kids left, so basically me against Mom. She has the other two under her thumb."

"You'll always have Grandma on your side," Elaina said. "And besides. It's only two years. Then you can apply to Berkeley and come and live with me and go to college. We'll be roommates again." She smiled over at Jess, showing her perfectly straight teeth.

"I'd like that," Jess said.

Elaina snapped open the middle armrest and pulled out a pack of Salems. "Light one up for me, okay?" She handed them to Jess.

"Mom would like this," Jess said with a grin, and both girls laughed.

Jess sat on the bed, forcing herself to stop the memory there. They'd been young and silly and full of life. Moments later, everything changed.

Jess wondered how different her life would have been if Elaina had lived. Would they have both moved to California and finished college there? Would she even be a lawyer? She'd become so serious and resentful those years after the crash that her entire outlook on life had changed. Yes, she'd had Jay to soften her a little, but she'd become determined to make something of herself. Jess had thought if she were a success, maybe it would make up for Elaina dying.

Of course, it hadn't.

A noise coming from downstairs brought Jess out of her thoughts. She glanced at the clock on the nightstand. 4:15. Her mother must be home.

Taking a deep breath, she closed her laptop and set it on the bed, then headed downstairs. Before she could enter the kitchen, her mother pushed through the door and stared hard at her.

"What have you done?"

CHAPTER ELEVEN

Christmas Eve 1970

Pat and June were working in the hardware store while Flori sat behind the counter, playing with a toy cash register. They usually kept the store open until 4:00 P.M. on Christmas Eve in case someone needed a last-minute gift or had a repair. Rhonda, their part-time employee, was working too, straightening products on the shelves.

Around three o'clock, Pat grabbed June's hand. "I want you to see something," he whispered so Flori wouldn't hear. "Rhonda can watch Flori for a few minutes."

June frowned. "Can't this wait until we close?"

Pat shook his head. "Come on, Juni-bug. Humor me." He nodded to Rhonda as they walked to the back room and put on their coats and boots. The snow had been endless this year, piled high everywhere around town.

"Where are we going?" June asked as they stepped into his truck. She was glad she'd worn slacks to work that day, otherwise her legs would be cold.

"You'll see," he said with a mischievous grin.

June sighed but didn't ask any more questions. She was thinking of the dinner she had to start once they returned home, and Pat still had to run to the farm and cut down a Christmas tree.

Pat drove down the street and several blocks later, pulled up to the old Victorian house on the corner and parked.

June was confused. "Why are we here?"

"Just follow me," Pat said. He stepped out of the truck and came around to help June down. It had snowed the night before, and although the rest of the neighborhood had shoveled their sidewalks, the walkway in front of the vacant Victorian still had snow piled up.

June trudged alongside Pat as he led her to the rickety picket fence surrounding the house. It had certainly seen better days. She turned to her husband. "Why are we here?"

"You know how when we walk by this house on the way to the city park, we say we wish we could restore her and bring her back to life?" Pat asked.

"Yes," June said.

"Well, I hope you meant it because this old lady is now ours." Pat smiled wide. "Merry Christmas, Juni-bug!"

June's mouth dropped open, and then she clamped it shut. She thought she'd heard wrong. "What?"

Pat took her gloved hands in his. "It's ours now. I put a down payment on it, and we can move in as soon as we clean it up a little inside."

June stared from Pat to the house. She'd always loved this house. She remembered when the Harpers had lived there and kept it up with fresh paint and a mowed lawn. At Christmas, they'd decorate it with lights that made it look like a gingerbread house. Watching it fall into disrepair over the years had made her sad. Mr. Harper's wife had died, and he'd lost interest in the house and moved away. No one wanted a house this size, so it sat unloved.

"It's ours? Really?" June asked, excitement growing inside her.

"It's all ours, sweetie," Pat said. He looked so happy he was nearly glowing.

June squealed with delight and hugged Pat. "I can't believe it! Can we go inside?"

Pat produced a ring of keys. "We sure can."

They opened the small gate and made their way through the high snow. June's boots filled with the cold, icy snow, but she didn't care. She was excited to see the house they would soon call home.

On the porch, Pat brushed the pile of snow aside with his boot so he could open the screen door. Then he unlocked the door, and they stepped inside. Pat produced a flashlight from his coat pocket and turned it on so June could look around.

"The power isn't on since no one lives here," he said. "But I was assured that it worked fine. And there is a central heating system, so we won't have to have a fire in every room."

June stared at him. "I never thought about that. Thank goodness the Harpers put in a furnace." She gazed around the room. The living room was large with a big bay window that let in the afternoon light. Behind it was a space where a good-sized dining room table could sit, and a built-in hutch was on the wall. The hardwood floors were scratched, and the walls needed a clean coat of paint. She looked over to the left where the staircase ran up along the wall. Again, the treads of the stairs were pretty scratched up.

"It's going to be a lot of work restoring this house," Pat said.

"We need to sand and stain the floors, paint the walls, and do a lot of touchups. Mr. Harper rented the place out for a bit to a family of five, and it got beat up pretty badly."

"That's okay," June said, touching his arm lightly. "We can make this place our own."

"That's the spirit," Pat said.

June went inside the kitchen. Her heart dropped. The appliances were old, and the tile counters were cracked in places. The sink had rust stains, and the linoleum floor was peeling up in places. "I'm sure we could fix this kitchen and make it cheerful again," she said, making herself believe her words.

"Of course we can," Pat said. "I'll bet there're hardwoods under that old linoleum, and we can paint the cabinets and buy new countertops. It'll take time, but we can shine this kitchen right up."

June turned and smiled at her husband. He was right. It would take a lot of work, but they could do it.

They toured the entire house, and June was surprised at how big it was. Once again, her heart fell. "Are you sure we need such a large house?" she asked. "There's only the three of us."

"It's big, that's for certain, but you just wait and see, Juni-bug. There are only three of us now but think of the years to come. Flori can have friends over, running all over the house, and someday she'll marry, and we'll have grandchildren scurrying about. This house will be able to hold everyone. It'll be our forever home."

June's heart filled with love for her husband. He was right. They would someday fill this house with family and friends and all the love they could give. Excitedly, she put her arm through his and turned him around toward the bay window in the living room.

"We'll put our Christmas tree right there each year and decorate it and tell the story of our first Christmas together when you gave me my star necklace," she said. "And we'll have family dinners in the dining room, and Flori and I and our granddaughters will all work together in the kitchen baking cookies and pies. I can see it all." She squeezed Pat's arm, and he kissed her sweetly.

"Merry Christmas, Juni-bug," he said.

"Merry Christmas, sweetie," she said back.

They left the house and headed back to the store so they could get Flori and celebrate their best Christmas ever.

Chapter Twelve

2022

Jess stood stock still, staring at her mother. "What?"

Florence moved a step closer. She still had her boots and coat on. "What have you done? Skyler called Rick at the store and asked him to bring new deadbolts for the doors and change her locks. When I got on the phone to ask her why she said she was divorcing Chris and she'd explain later." Florence stared at Jess with accusing eyes. "You had to have done something to make her do this."

Jess was dumbfounded. She couldn't believe her mother would blame her for the disintegration of Skyler's marriage. "Me? I didn't do anything. Blame Chris if you have to blame someone. He's been cheating on Skyler for over six months."

Her mother's face went blank while she digested this new information. Then her lips tightened again. "Whatever is going on between them has nothing to do with you. Did you talk her into leaving Chris? At Christmastime? What do you think this will do to the children? Having their dad locked out of their house the day before Christmas Eve. Did you even stop to think about that?"

Anger boiled up inside Jess. Her mother may have blamed her for Elaina's death, but she certainly wasn't going to blame her for Skyler's failing marriage. "If you're asking if I gave her advice, then yes, I did. She's the one who's had enough of her cheating husband. She came to me for help—I didn't give her unsolicited advice. I'm not going to see my little sister get cheated out of what she deserves by a conniving husband."

"You shouldn't have gotten involved at all," Florence said. She walked over to the hall closet and hung up her coat, then took off her boots. "Look at the trouble you've caused now." Florence turned back to her. "If Skyler was having marital problems for that long, don't you think I'd have known?"

Jess crossed her arms. "Obviously, you didn't notice it because it was happening right here in this tiny town under your nose."

Florence walked up to Jess, pointing her finger at her. "Don't you dare say I'm not paying attention to my own daughter. Skyler and I are close. She would have told me if she was unhappy in her marriage."

Jess laughed. "Close? Are you kidding me? If that was true, then yes, you would have known. You'd know a lot more about what's going on with all your kids. But you don't. Grandma was always open to listening to everyone. She would have paid attention and known. But you only see what you want to see."

Her mother stared at her for one long moment. "You shouldn't have come home," she said, her tone even. "All you've done is complain and argue with me. How dare you think I don't know what's going on with my own family. You're the one who doesn't stay in touch. You're the one who disappeared after your grandmother died and stayed away. Maybe you were right to stay away."

Jess's heart clenched. Her own mother was telling her she shouldn't have come home. Pulling up as much pride as she could, Jess said, "Maybe you're right. We both would have been better off if I hadn't come home. You're certainly never going to change. You're always going to believe the worst of me. Fine. But don't you dare blame me for Skyler's problems. Those are clearly on Chris." Jess ran up the stairs before her mother could say another word. She grabbed her coat and purse and ran back down to the door.

"Where are you going?" Florence yelled.

"Anywhere but here," Jess said. She walked outside, closed the door, and headed to her car.

Once Jess got behind the wheel, she had no idea where she would go. It was already getting dark out, and she hadn't grabbed her suitcase, so she couldn't drive home to Minneapolis. Besides, Skyler needed her for the next few days.

Jess drove in circles, forcing tears back. Her mother could be difficult, but to blame her for all the misfortune going on in their lives was ridiculous. Still, having your own mother say you shouldn't have come home hurt. It hurt deeply.

Jess thought about going to Skyler's house, but there was enough drama going on there already. She didn't want to put a damper on Mandy and Rick's night either. She could go to the small hotel in town, but it wasn't the nicest place to stay. Finally, she went once again to the one place she'd feel welcome.

Jess drove into the parking lot of The Pier and turned off her car. She quickly checked her eyes in the visor mirror to make sure her mascara hadn't run, then stepped out of the car and walked quickly inside. The place was busy, but she brushed past tables of locals and headed to the other side of the bar. The moment Jay saw her, he came over.

"Wow. You're becoming a regular," he teased, but then his expression turned serious. "What's wrong?"

Jess sat down and tried hard not to cry. "I had a big blowout with my mom," she said. "It was awful. I didn't know where to go."

Jay glanced around the bar, then back at Jess. "Come on. Let's go to my office so you can have privacy." He guided her to the back room and to the nook where his desk sat. "Here. Sit down and relax. I'll let my assistant know I'll be off the floor for a while."

Jess watched Jay leave and felt terrible again. She really was messing up everyone's lives. She wished now that she had packed her bag and left for home.

Jay returned with a drink and handed it to her. "Rum and Coke. I think you need it."

She smiled. "Thanks. You're not wrong about that. Listen, I'm sorry I came here and interrupted your night. It seems that's all I've done since I got to town. I had nowhere to go."

Jay looked at her seriously. "You are not interrupting my night. I told you I'm here for you, and I meant it. What can I do? Do you want to talk?"

She shook her head. "No. Not here. I hate asking, but can I stay at your place tonight? I don't think I could stand to face my mother anytime soon."

He smiled. "No problem. Here." Jay reached into his pocket and pulled out his keys. "This is for the side door. Go in, watch TV, and make yourself at home. Have you eaten since that plate of fries earlier?"

"No. But I'm not hungry." She took a sip of her drink.

"Wait here a few more minutes. I'll send a wrap home with

you," Jay said. He pointed to the drink. "And no more of that on an empty stomach."

Jess sat there waiting for Jay, replaying the argument with her mother in her head. Was she the crazy one? How could her mother think she'd want her sister to divorce her husband if they weren't having problems? Her mother always did this to her—she made her second guess everything. That was why she needed Grandma June. She could calm Florence down and make her see the truth. Well, on everything except Elaina's death.

Picking up her phone, Jess called Skyler to check on her.

"Hi, how are you doing?" Jess asked when her sister answered the phone.

"I'm okay. Rick came and changed the locks. I did what you said and put some of Chris's things in a bag and set it on the porch. He was just here trying to get in," Skyler said.

"How'd that go?" Jess asked.

"He pounded on the door to let him in but stopped when I called his phone and said he'd scare the kids. So, he picked up his bag and left."

"Did you tell him anything else?" Jess asked.

"I told him to get a lawyer. He looked angry, which I find annoying. He's the one who cheated, not me. If he's angry, it should be at himself," Skyler said.

"I'm sorry this is all happening, especially at Christmas," Jess said.

"Thanks. But it's not your fault. I've been scared to do anything all these months, but now that I have someone on my side, I feel so much better," Skyler said.

Jess winced. "Tell me the truth. Did I talk you into divorcing Chris?"

"What? No. Of course not. You just gave me the strength to do what needed to be done."

"Well, just so you know, Mom is blaming me for you two splitting. She and I had a big fight. I wouldn't be surprised if she calls you and tries to talk you into staying with Chris," Jess said.

"I'll set her straight," Skyler said. "This is about me, not her. She just never sees the truth."

"That's for sure," Jess said.

"Jess? Do you think I'll ruin Christmas for the kids? That's what Chris said on the phone. I mean, they're still young. If we're civil about it at least until after Christmas, it should be okay, shouldn't it?"

Jess's heart went out to her. Skyler went from sounding self-assured to sounding like her baby sister. "I think they'll be fine. Like you said, they're still young. Don't make a big deal about him not being there for Christmas. It would be worse if you two were together, arguing the whole time."

"I think that too. Thanks, Jess. And don't worry about Mom. I'll calm her down," Skyler said.

As Jess hung up, she had to laugh at Skyler's last words. Everyone was always catering to her mother. That's why she acted like the spoiled person she was.

"Here you go," Jay said, bringing in a bag. "Sorry it took so long. Go to the house and eat this, okay? I'll be home in a little bit."

All the stress of the day washed over Jess. She stood and hugged Jay, nearly crushing the food bag between them. "Thank you," she whispered in his ear. "I needed someone who understood me tonight."

After she'd pulled away, he smiled at her and kissed her on

the forehead. "Anytime."

As Jess looked up into his soft blue eyes, memories of the many times he'd comforted her in the past rushed over her. Jay had always been there for her when they were teens. How had she been so stupid to let him go?

He walked her out to her car and stood there, watching as she drove away. Her best memories after Elaina's death had included Jay. Always Jay.

* * *

Jess parked in Jay's driveway and walked into the house through the kitchen door. She set the bag of food in the fridge and pulled out a bottle of water to drink. She wasn't hungry. She was worn out from the day's events.

Before dropping onto the sofa, Jess plugged in the Christmas tree lights. She smiled. The scent of pine surrounded her, and the lights made her happy. Laying down, she stared at the tree, remembering all of her childhood Christmases. Decorating the tree as a family on Christmas Eve while listening to her Grandma June tell the story of when Grandpa Pat gave her the star necklace. Drinking hot chocolate the next morning as they all sat around the tree, opening presents. The year Santa gave her a bicycle. The year she begged for a CD boombox and finally got it. Jess had always loved that they had Christmas together. Some of her grade-school friends had said it was weird that their grandparents lived with them, but Jess had loved it. Her grandmother had always been there for her with an understanding ear and never judged her. Jess didn't know what she or Elaina would have done without their grandmother's calming presence influencing Florence to stop and listen. Florence was a doer. She rarely had time to listen to childish nonsense or teenage angst. But Grandma June did listen, and for that, Jess would always be grateful.

Of course, there were unhappy memories of Christmas too. The first Christmas after Elaina's death had been hard. They'd put up her stocking because the mantel had looked empty without it. Instead of gifts, they had all put loving notes inside it about how much they each missed her. And the Christmas after Grandpa Pat died in 2017. They'd missed his silly jokes and gentle ways. That year, Grandma had recited her story about the Christmas charm with tears in her eyes. It had been a tough year for all of them.

Jess had grown so comfortable on the sofa that she'd almost fallen asleep when her phone buzzed. She glanced at it and saw it was her dad calling.

"Hi, Dad," she said, sounding groggy.

"Hey, Pumpkin. I heard you and your mom had a little tiff. Are you okay?"

Jess chuckled. "A tiff? Is that what she called it? More like a knockdown, drag-out fight."

"Yeah. She said it was bad. Are you over at Jay's?" Thomas asked.

"I am. But please don't tell mom. I need some time to myself after what she said," Jess told him.

"I get it, honey. I really do. But maybe it would be better if you came home and you two talked it out. It won't go away until you do."

"I can't, Dad. You weren't there. She really hit a nerve. I'm not even sure I'm staying for Christmas. Mom said it might be better if I weren't here," Jess said.

"Oh, honey. She didn't mean it. She's just upset about

Skyler's problems and her not knowing anything about them. It's been a tough three years since her mother died. Your grandmother used to help her through times like this. Your mother is a little lost, that's all. She's not very good at navigating emotions."

"She's lost? She sounded pretty sure of herself this afternoon. Grandma's passing was hard on all of us, Dad. Mom needs to be more understanding of everyone's feelings, not just her own. Besides, you know it's more than that. Mom is never going to forgive me for Elaina's death." Jess was near tears. She felt raw after what her mother had said, and she couldn't just give her a pass like everyone else did.

"Oh, honey," Thomas said gently. "Your mother never blamed you for Elaina's death. It wasn't your fault. Elaina was driving. Everyone knows that. I really think it's time you and your mother work through this."

"I can't, Dad. I'm sorry. I can't take another thing today."

"Okay. I understand," Thomas said. "I love you, honey. I hope you'll join us for dinner tomorrow night. We all need each other."

"I love you, too, Dad," Jess said as tears fell down her cheeks. Why was it easy to tell him she loved him, but she couldn't get the words out for her mother? Probably because her mother never said those words to her, either.

After saying goodnight, Jess hung up. It was only ten o'clock, and she was so emotionally drained that she didn't have the energy to get off the sofa and find a guest room to sleep in. She just lay there, staring at the Christmas tree, trying to figure out how her life had come to this. She was a hard worker and a good person. She loved her sister and brother and her niece and nephew. She adored her father and had loved her grandparents. Why was her relationship with her mother so difficult? Why did she always feel like she was a terrible person when she came home?

Jess heard the kitchen door open and footsteps across the hardwood floor. Jay's smiling face appeared over the sofa, but his expression changed when he saw her tears.

"Hey, what's wrong?" He hurried around the sofa and pulled her into a hug.

"Everything," Jess said, no longer able to stop crying. "My mother hates me, my father thinks I'm being too hard on her, my sister's life is falling apart, and Rick and Mandy want nothing more than to have a baby. But here I am, in the middle of it all, feeling like somehow, it's all my fault."

Jay pulled back with wide eyes. "How on earth could all that be your fault?" He drew her close again, not waiting for an answer. He just held her as she cried, rubbing her back with his hand. It was all she needed, and somehow, Jay knew that.

"You're tired and stressed and need some sleep," Jay said soothingly. "Let's get you to bed." He stood, pulling her up with him, and wrapped his arm around her waist. Too tired to protest, Jess walked up the stairs beside him. When they stopped at the guest room, she wiped her tears with the back of her hand.

"I don't want to be alone," Jess said, looking over at Jay. "Can I sleep with you tonight?"

He gave her a small smile. "Absolutely. What are friends for?"

His words made her laugh despite her tears. Together, they walked down the hallway to his room. Jay pulled back the comforter and sheets, then walked to the dresser and grabbed an oversized T-shirt from one of the drawers.

"Here. You can wear this." He nodded toward the attached bathroom.

"Thanks." Jess went into the bathroom and changed, then stared at herself in the mirror. Her mascara had run down her cheeks, and her eyes were red and puffy. Grabbing a tissue, she wet it and wiped away the mascara. She was so tired, that was all she could manage. She returned to the bedroom where Jay had already changed and was lying in bed. Jess joined him, pulling the sheets up over her.

Jay turned out the light on his nightstand. "Goodnight." He leaned over and kissed her gently on the cheek.

"Thank you," Jess whispered, feeling close to tears again. "I needed a friend tonight."

"I'm always here for you," he said.

Jess reached behind her and took his hand. Pulling it gently, she made her wishes known to him without words. Jay rolled over and wrapped his arm around her, curling his warm body next to hers.

"Goodnight," she said softly. She felt safe and warm, just as she'd always felt when she was with Jay.

CHAPTER THIRTEEN

Christmas Eve 1983

June was very excited this Christmas Eve. Every Christmas was special, but this one was even more so. As she prepared the turkey, stuffing, and gravy, she also thought of what she would say to Florence and her new husband when they came to dinner.

The years had gone by quickly for June and Pat after they'd bought their house and began the long job of remodeling it and filling it with beautiful furniture. Both happy and sad events had happened to their family. Pat's father had died not long after they'd bought the Victorian house, and soon after, his mother had grown ill and passed. The farm and house had been sold, and the money and possessions had been doled out between Pat and his older brother. June cherished the beautiful maple dining room table that sat in their home, which had belonged to Pat's parents. The extra money from the farm had helped them grow their business and make much-needed repairs to their house. What was once a run-down old home was now a beautiful Victorian that stood proudly on the corner. Each Christmas, they decorated it with lights and it shone brightly in the neighborhood. June and Pat were very proud of all they'd accomplished.

Their most treasured accomplishment, though, was their daughter, Florence. She'd grown into a lovely young woman, doing well in school. Just this past June, she'd married Thomas Paxton, a boy she'd gone to school with and who'd worked in the hardware store alongside Pat. They adored Tom because of his kind and generous nature. The couple had taken up residence in the old apartment above the hardware store, and Thomas began working there full-time. June had started teaching Florence how to do the books for the business, too. Pat and June were thrilled that they would someday pass down the business to the next generation.

"Mom? Are you in the kitchen?" Florence walked through the swinging door carrying a freshly made apple pie. She glowed with youth and happiness.

"How are you feeling?" June asked her daughter.

"I'm fine, Mom. Don't fuss. Women have babies all the time," Flori said, brushing off her mother's concern.

June smiled. Her daughter would be a mother in a few short months, and she couldn't wait to be a grandmother.

The two women moved around the kitchen almost as if in harmony. They'd worked together cooking since Florence was a child, and they could practically read each other's minds. While other mothers would complain to June about their teenage daughters' attitudes or how they no longer saw them when they were grown, June had always been thankful she and Flori had a good relationship. They confided in each other much as friends would, and even through her teen years, Flori talked to her mother about everything. Now that Flori was grown and married, they were more like best friends than mother and daughter, and June cherished that.

The kitchen door opened, and in walked Pat and Thomas, their coats covered in snow.

"It's really coming down out there," Pat said. "I set the tree on the front porch hoping the snow would fall off before I brought it in."

"I'll get the plastic carpet runner, and you can carry it in and set it up," June said, still excited to decorate the tree after all these years. She hurried to the hall closet and pulled out the long runner she had for snowy days.

"I'll shake it off before bringing it in," Pat said. Thomas followed him outside, and the two men lifted the tree, one on each end, and shook it. Then they carried it in and placed it on the plastic runner.

Florence walked into the living room and sat on the arm of the sofa. "The tree stand is in that box." She pointed to an old box sitting on the living room floor. Thomas took off his boots first, then hung his coat before getting the stand. Soon, the two men connected the stand and set the tree up in front of the bay window. June placed towels under it in case it dripped water.

"Beautiful," Pat said, smiling over at his wife. "It should be dry enough to decorate after dinner."

Thomas insisted on helping June bring the dinner to the table so Florence could sit. "You're on your feet too much," he told her. "The doctor said you need to rest more."

Florence rolled her eyes but did as he said. "It is nice to sit," she admitted.

Finally, they all sat down and passed the many dishes of delicious food. Once they started eating, June couldn't contain her excitement any longer. She glanced over at Pat, and he smiled and nodded. Taking a deep breath, June spoke up.

"We wanted to ask you two something tonight," June said, feeling nervous. She hoped Flori and Thomas wouldn't think she was being pushy.

Florence looked up at her mother. "What?"

"I will completely understand if your answer is no. I mean, you are still newlyweds, and you're expecting a child soon. I know your privacy is very important." June looked at Flori, who stared back, looking confused.

Pat chuckled. "What your mother is trying to say is we'd like it very much if you'd consider moving into the house with us."

Both Thomas and Florence stared at him with wide eyes.

"It's just that we have this big house," June said in a rush. "And I know you'll need help once the baby arrives. It would be nice if you were here so I could help. But also, we'd definitely respect your privacy."

"Are you sure about this?" Florence asked her mother. "Would you really want a newborn in the house, crying at all hours of the night? And us underfoot all the time?"

June smiled wide. "Honestly, I'd love it." She reached over and took Pat's hand. "We were never able to have more children, and I want so much to enjoy my grandchild—or grandchildren—if you decide to have more. This house was meant to hold a big family, and we'd love it if you'd want to join us here."

Florence looked over at her husband, then back at her mom. "How would that work?"

June grew excited. "We thought we'd turn the den downstairs into our bedroom. There's a bathroom right next to it, so it would be like having our own little suite. Then, you could have the big bedroom upstairs and use the other three for the children." She held her breath, hoping Flori would agree.

"Of course, you two can discuss this between yourselves before you decide," Pat added. "It's not a spur-of-the-moment decision."

Thomas reached over and patted Florence's hand, and she smiled wide. "We don't have to think about it," she said. "We'd love to come and live here."

"Really?" June couldn't believe her ears.

"Yes," Florence said, tears filling her eyes. "I've missed living at home, and I'll need help with the baby. I'd feel so much better if we were here."

"Oh, I'm so excited!" June hurried to the other side of the table and hugged her daughter. "This will be wonderful. And I promise we won't meddle in your lives or tell you how to parent your children. We just want to be a part of everything."

"I know you do, Mom," Florence said. "And I want you to be there for everything. Like you said, this house is big and should be filled with family. Just don't be surprised if it gets too full." She laughed.

"The more the merrier," June said. She sat down again but was too excited to eat. That was when she noticed how quiet Thomas was. Calming down, she said to her son-in-law, "If at any time this becomes too much, we'll understand if you'll want to get a place of your own."

Thomas smiled over at her. "I know this is what Florence wants, and I'm fine with it. You've all been so good to me since the very first day I started working at the store. I'm sure it will work out fine."

"Of course it will," Pat said cheerily. "This is what family is all about."

That evening after dinner, they all talked and joked as they decorated the tree and then sat in the living room, eating pie by the light of the tree. By this time next year, June would have a beautiful baby grandson or granddaughter to share their holiday traditions with. June's heart was full.

Chapter Fourteen

December 24, 2022

Jess awoke slowly to the smell of fresh coffee. The sun was peeking through the curtains as she rolled over. She'd slept so soundly that she felt completely rested for the first time in months.

"Good morning," Jay said as he entered the room with a tray in his hands.

Jess looked up and smiled. He was showered and dressed, and she could smell a hint of his spicy aftershave. What smelled even better was the coffee he'd brought in. "You're a lifesaver," she said, sitting up in bed as Jay came around and sat on his side.

"It's about time you woke up. You city girls sleep in late," he teased.

"Late? What time is it?" She gratefully accepted the mug of hot coffee he handed her.

"Ten. I let you sleep in. I think you needed it," he said. "And it was tempting to stay in bed with you, but I have to open the bar by eleven."

She smiled over at him and was rewarded with one of his mischievous grins that made his blue eyes sparkle. It would have been nice to wake up slowly beside Jay. But then, it may have turned into something more than she was able to handle. She had enough problems dealing with her family right now.

"Here. Have a pastry. They're homemade," Jay said. He picked one up and took a bite. "Apple cinnamon. Yum."

"Homemade, huh?" Jess lifted one and took a bite. "These are yummy. But who actually made them?"

Jay gave her a hurt look. "I did." Then he smiled. "Me and the Pillsbury Dough Boy."

Jess laughed. "They're delicious. Thanks." She wanted to lean over and kiss him but stopped herself. It seemed like such a normal thing to do, yet it might mean a lot more than a friendly kiss to Jay, and she didn't want to lead him on. Sleeping in his bed last night was confusing enough.

Jay stood. "Well, you relax and enjoy your breakfast while I go and slave away at work."

She sighed. "It's going to be a tough day. I guess I'll have to make a truce with my mother somehow and play along at being nice."

"Oh, about that. Your mother invited me to Christmas Eve dinner tonight," Jay said.

Jess's brows rose. "Really? What did you say?"

"I said yes, of course. Do you think I'd turn down a home-cooked Christmas dinner?"

She shook her head. "From the way mom talked to me yesterday, you may get dinner and a show. So be warned."

He laughed, then bent down and kissed her chastely on the cheek. "See you later."

Jess watched him walk out the door, wondering what the

kiss meant. Then she wondered why she was analyzing everything. It was a friendly peck, nothing more.

After finishing her coffee, Jess went downstairs, put their mugs in the dishwasher, and covered the plate of turnovers with Saran wrap. She looked around the kitchen, admiring the new cabinets and countertops. It really was a beautiful kitchen. In fact, Jay had created a nice, cozy space in this older home, making it modern but still warm and inviting. He had really good taste. Just one more thing to make him seem perfect in her eyes.

After Jess finished in the kitchen, she returned upstairs and put on yesterday's clothes. She figured her mother was at the hardware store until at least two, so she could go over, shower, and change quickly. Then, Jess would go to Skyler's shop to see how she was faring.

An hour later, Jess was back in her car, parking in front of Skyler's shop. The town looked deserted, with only a few cars around. There were no customers in the shop when Jess entered, and Skyler was the only one standing behind the counter.

"Hi," Jess said, walking up to the counter. "How are you doing today?"

Skyler smiled. She looked much better compared to the day before. She wore a creamy white angora sweater and a black pencil skirt with tall black heels. Her hair was pulled up in a messy bun that wasn't messy at all, and her makeup was impeccable. "I'm doing a lot better," she said, giving Jess a hug. "Thanks to you."

"Don't give me any credit. You made the decision to change your life, not me. I just gave you advice," Jess said.

"Yes, but you also gave me the courage to do it. I've been letting Chris slide all these months because I was scared. Now,

I'm relieved that I finally made the decision to split. Thank you for that."

"As long as it's what you truly want," Jess said.

"It is." Skyler looked determined. "And I'm not stressing about it anymore. Everything will be fine in the end."

"Wow," Jess said, impressed. "What made you become so decisive?"

"Actually, I decided I was doing the right thing after I talked with mom last night," Skyler said, grinning. "Can you believe that?"

"No, I can't," Jess said. "Was she actually encouraging?"

Skyler laughed. "No. Not at all. She told me I was making a mistake pushing Chris away, especially during the holidays. She said I was just tired and emotional, and maybe if Chris and I could go away together after the new year, we could fix our problems. She even offered to babysit so we could have a vacation together."

"Are you kidding me?" Jess asked, incensed. She couldn't believe her mother would think a vacation together would fix his cheating problem.

Skyler shook her head. "Nope. She actually said that. When I told her that wasn't going to happen, then she blamed me for not trying harder to keep my marriage together. She said I'd ruin the kids' holidays for the rest of their lives. She sounded crazy."

"What did you say?" Jess asked.

"I calmly told her the kids would be fine as long as we all behaved normally and didn't make a big deal about Chris's absence. I also asked her to not mention any of this tonight when we're all together. This is my life, and I need to make the decisions I feel are best for my kids and me."

"Wow. I'm proud of you," Jess said. "You stood up to her."

"Yeah. But it didn't make her happy, that's for sure. She'll have to get used to the idea that I'm getting divorced. End of story."

"I'm glad you told her how it is. But it still won't be easy tonight," Jess said. "I'm still not sure I can stay. Maybe it would be best if I go home."

Skyler's brows scrunched together. "This is your home. You belong here just as much as any of us. Please don't leave, Jess. I need you for moral support. And I want you there for the children. They need to get to know you better. Mom can just suck it up and be nice."

Jess broke out laughing, and Skyler joined in. "What's happened to you?" Jess asked. "You never go against mom's wishes."

"I'm finally becoming the person I should have been years ago," Skyler said. Her face grew serious. "I know I was a lot younger than you and Elaina and that I don't understand what happened that day. But I hope you and mom can find a way to put that behind you and finally get along. I want you in my life."

Jess hugged Skyler. "I am in your life. And I'm not going anywhere. I'll 'suck it up' too and stay for Christmas."

"Good. That means a lot to me," Skyler said.

The bell on the door chimed, and both women looked up. Mandy walked in, smiling at them. "Am I interrupting anything?" she asked.

"Not at all," Jess said. "Aren't you busy either?"

"No. Not really. I have one of the other women working until three, and then we're closing. I just wanted to be open in case there were any last-minute drop-ins," Mandy said.

Skyler took a deep breath. "So, just so you know, I'm divorcing Chris. He won't be at the house tonight."

Mandy didn't look surprised. "I'm sorry to hear that, but that's why I came over. Florence called me earlier and was in a tizzy."

"Are you kidding me?" Jess said. "What did she say?"

"She said Skyler had lost her mind and was ruining her marriage, and Jess was helping her. She thought I could talk some sense into both of you." Mandy chuckled. "I tried to calm her down and said I'd come to talk to you. But honestly, I think you're doing the right thing." Mandy hesitated. "I've seen Chris out with his father's secretary a couple of times. I wouldn't have thought much of it since it was for lunch, but they just seemed a bit too cozy together."

"Why didn't you ever say anything?" Skyler asked.

"I'm sorry. But if I told you, then I'd have to tell Rick, too. And he would have gone off the rails. He's very protective of his little sister." Mandy smiled.

"I'm sorry to say, but Jay has seen them together at the bar, too, over the past few months," Jess said. "Chris hasn't been hiding his affair, that's for sure."

Skyler stood a little taller. "Well then, that just makes me more determined. I'm not imagining it—he's been cheating. So, I'm not going to feel guilty for breaking up our family. Because he's the one who broke us up, not me."

"I agree," Mandy said. "And I'm one-hundred percent behind you tonight and throughout the entire process."

Skyler stepped over and hugged Mandy. "Thank you. I'm going to need everyone's support."

"I'm not looking forward to tonight, that's for sure," Jess said. "I wish Grandma June was still with us. She'd know how to handle mom."

Skyler nodded. "Yeah. She had a way of talking to her so she'd listen. Mom always jumps to conclusions, but Grandma listened. I miss her a lot."

"Me too," Mandy said. "She always kept the peace. She made me feel welcomed in the family the first time Rick brought me home. Wow, that was a long time ago."

"It was," Jess said. "Despite everything, our family still has a lot of good memories too."

The women went their separate ways, and Jess got back into her car. She wasn't sure how the night would turn out, so she drove back to the house, packed her bag, and put it and her laptop bag into her car. She wanted to be ready in case she had to leave.

On her way out the door, Jess stared at the fake Christmas tree. Her Grandma June had always insisted on a real tree, and they'd set it up on Christmas Eve and decorate it after dinner. Jess knew her mother had also enjoyed that yearly ritual, so it made no sense why she changed everything and put up this fake tree with plastic ornaments. The more Jess stared at the tree, the more she hated it. Finally, she turned and walked out to her car.

Jess sat there, feeling lost. Normally, on Christmas Eve, she'd be in the kitchen helping Grandma June prepare dinner. But she didn't want to be alone with her mother when she came home, so she decided to visit Jay at The Pier.

Jay's face brightened from across the room when he saw Jess walk in. It was still lunchtime, but the place wasn't busy. Jess supposed that most people opted to go home early to start their celebrations rather than go out for lunch.

"Hey there," Jay said as Jess sat at the bar. "You just can't stay away from me." He grinned.

"That's right. You're all I have left in the world," Jess teased.

Jay frowned. "I'm not sure if that's a compliment or insult. Do you mean that I'm your last resort?"

She laughed. "No, not at all. In fact, I don't know what I would have done without you this week. And I've really enjoyed spending time with you."

That put a smile back on Jay's lips. "I'm glad to hear that. I've been enjoying your company, too. It brings back all the good memories."

Jess studied Jay for a moment. He was right. Being with him now was just as easy as it had been years ago. Sure, they'd been kids then and were madly in love with their whole lives ahead of them. But now, seeing everything as an adult, Jess was surprised that their relationship was still easy and comfortable.

"Want a drink? Lunch? What can I get you?" Jay asked.

"How about a salad?" Jess said. "There will be a lot of food tonight—if I stay for dinner—so I don't want to fill up too much now."

"Sure thing," Jay said. "Oh, by the way. Your mother called me a while ago. She was wondering if I knew where you were and if you were going to come home for dinner tonight. You should call her."

Jess rolled her eyes. "Really? She bothered you when she could have just called my cell phone? She was the one who was rude to me, so she can call me herself."

Jay shook his head. "You are both very stubborn. Always have been."

"Hey. Don't you go and say that too," Jess said.

"Say what? That you're both stubborn?"

"Yes. What you're really saying is I'm just like my mother.

My dad already told me that. I don't need you telling me that, too." Jess was growing angry. She was nothing like her mother. Just because she stood up to her when no one else would didn't make her like Florence.

"Whoa there. I never said you were just like your mother. Do I look like an idiot?" Jay grinned. "I know better than to tell any woman that. But you are stubborn. Even you have to admit that."

Jess bit her lip to stop herself from saying anything that would turn Jay against her too. "Well, okay. Yeah. I'm a lawyer. We're supposed to be stubborn and fight our case. But at least I listen to people."

"I'll get your salad," he said. "And just a word of advice. Don't be so hard on your mother. Put yourself in her place. She not only lost her oldest daughter years ago, but she lost her mother not long ago too. She's probably just trying to figure out her life without your grandmother."

"I get that," Jess said. "But I lost my sister and my best friend when Elaina died, and my mother won't acknowledge that. It was hard for me. Elaina and I had plans that fell to pieces the day she died. It still hurts."

Jay leaned against the bar and placed his hand over hers. "I know it does. That's why you should be able to understand why your mother is hurting."

Jess frowned. "Why?"

Jay leaned in closer to her. "Because the day your grandmother died, your mother lost her best friend too. They were so close. Your mother just hasn't learned how to navigate without your grandmother. She's lost." He patted her hand and headed to the kitchen to get her food.

Jess hadn't thought of it that way. Her mom and Grandma

June had been close, just like best friends. Of course her mother was hurting. But so were the rest of them. Grandma June was the one who'd held the family together.

As Jess thought about what Jay had said, she also thought about the tree again. The tradition of decorating a live tree with Grandma June's ornaments was just as important as her telling the story of her Christmas star necklace. Traditions were what kept families together and helped them stay strong. Losing that was like losing yet another piece of her grandmother.

"One salad, coming up," Jay said, setting it down in front of Jess. "What would you like to drink?"

"Just a Coke," she said absently. Staring at her salad, Jess had an idea. Her mother wasn't going to like it, but it was something she had to do.

"Would you be able to pick up a Christmas tree before coming to the house for dinner tonight?" Jess asked Jay.

"Uh, yeah. I could. Why?"

Jess smiled. "Because tonight we're going to have a good old-fashioned family Christmas just as it should be."

CHAPTER FIFTEEN

December 22, 2017

June sat beside the bed where Pat lay sleeping. It was early afternoon, and the house was quiet. Florence and Thomas were working at the store so they had the house to themselves.

Pat's breathing was ragged as he struggled to breathe. Two years before, he'd been diagnosed with lung cancer. The doctors had no idea how he'd gotten it. Pat had never been a smoker, although he grew up in a home where his father smoked. He'd gone through the treatments, but it had spread, nevertheless. At seventy-eight years old, his body could no longer fight the inevitable. After a lengthy consultation between him, his doctor, and June, Pat declined any further treatment. He wanted to live out what was left of his life without the side effects of cancer drugs.

Now, his frail body was struggling with every breath. His eyelids fluttered open as he coughed, and June helped him sit up and fluffed the pillows behind him. He had an oxygen machine, so she handed him the mask, but he refused it with a wave of his hand.

"I'll get you some fresh water," she said, hurrying out of their bedroom and to the kitchen. She filled a glass pitcher with filtered water from the fridge and took a clean glass from the cupboard. Then she rushed back to his side.

"You're too good to me," he croaked, accepting a drink of water. His coughing had settled down, and he was breathing easier.

"You deserve it," June said, smiling.

Pat smiled back. He had very little hair now, and his face was thinner, but his kind eyes still warmed when he smiled. "It's almost Christmas," he said, staring out the bedroom door toward the living room. "I suppose Thomas will get a tree soon."

"On Christmas Eve, as always," June said. Then she had a thought. "Should we put it up a little earlier? You always enjoyed the smell of the fresh pine."

Pat shook his head slowly. "No. Keep the tradition. Traditions are important. Will Jess be home soon?"

June's heart warmed at hearing Jess's name. She didn't believe in having a favorite grandchild, but if she had one, it would be Jess. "She's coming tomorrow and staying through the new year. Maybe you two can play a few hands of Gin Rummy."

"I'd like that." Pat closed his eyes again, and June tucked the blankets around him. She knew he always felt cold these days. Sitting back in her chair, she opened her book again. It was hard concentrating on the story because she heard every ragged breath. But June knew Pat wouldn't want her to worry. He'd want her to go about her life as if all were fine.

It wasn't easy, though. June worried about the day she'd lose her beloved husband. They'd been together for so long and had done so much as a team, she couldn't imagine life without him.

"Juni-bug?" Pat's voice broke the silence again. June immediately set her book down and leaned toward him.

"I'm here, sweetie," she said softly.

"I want you all to enjoy the holidays no matter what happens," Pat said, each word a struggle. "It's little Aaron's first Christmas, and it should be a happy one."

"We will," June promised, although if the worst happened and Pat left them, then it would be hard.

"Remember our first Christmas?" Pat asked, smiling.

June reached for his hand and held it gently. "Of course I do," she said. "You brought home that beautiful tree that you'd cut down at the farm, and we had a string of lights and a few ornaments I'd bought at the dime store to decorate it with. It was perfect."

"And I bought you that beautiful star necklace," he said in barely a whisper. "To celebrate our first of many Christmases together."

"Yes, you did. And I've treasured it all these years," June said.

"Are you wearing it?" Pat asked, turning his head toward her.

June reached up to her neck and realized she wasn't. "I forgot to put it on. I'll get it." She went to the dresser and picked up the necklace from her small wooden jewelry box. She lifted the necklace and hooked it around her neck before returning to Pat's side. "I have it on."

He stared at the necklace for a long time without speaking. Finally, Pat said, "There. Everything is as it should be." He closed his eyes.

Tears filled June's eyes as she watched her husband sleep. "I love you, Pat," she said softly.

"I love you, Juni-bug," Pat whispered. It was so soft, that June almost thought she'd imagined it.

* * *

On Christmas Eve, Thomas brought home a fresh tree that was so full and beautiful that they all agreed it was the loveliest tree they'd ever had.

"Grandpa would have loved this tree," Jess said, her eyes filling with tears.

June walked up to her granddaughter and patted her back. "He wanted us all to enjoy Christmas, even if he wasn't with us. I know it's hard, but we must do as he wished."

Jess nodded, as did Florence and Skyler. They'd put on a brave face for their grandfather.

Pat had passed away quietly the afternoon June had put on her Christmas necklace. She'd been by his side the entire time. The family decided to wait until after Christmas to have his funeral because June had told them that was what he'd wanted.

That year, despite their great loss, the family spent the evening decorating the tree as they shared stories among themselves of past Christmases with Grandpa Pat. As hard as it was, June knew it was exactly what Pat would have wanted, and everything was as it should be.

CHAPTER SIXTEEN

Christmas Eve 2022

Jess stayed away from the house until she knew the rest of the family would be there. She'd gone to Jay's and changed into a soft red sweater and jeans, hoping she looked more festive than she felt. When she heard Jay's truck pull into his driveway, she slipped on her coat and met him outdoors.

"Did you get the tree?" she asked, glancing around to the back of his truck.

"I did. But I don't think your mother is going to like this."

"I'm not doing this to make her mad. I'm doing it because it's our tradition, and that's important to our family," Jess said.

Jay grimaced. "Well, hopefully she doesn't get mad at me for helping." He went inside to change into nicer clothes, then put his boots back on. "Ready?"

"Ready as I'll ever be," Jess said.

Together, they carried the tree around the front of Jay's house and over to Jess's. They shook the tree of excess snow before stepping up on the front porch. Then Jess opened the front door.

"There you are," her father said cheerfully, rising from his favorite chair. "Is Jay with you?"

Jess nodded. She glanced around, noting that Skyler and the kids were there as well as Mandy and Rick. She figured her mother was in the kitchen. "We have a surprise," Jess said. She stepped out the door again and she and Jay carried in the tree.

"A tree!" Aaron squealed happily, and his little sister copied him, adding to the noise. The adults in the room only stared at it, wide-eyed.

"It's Christmas Eve," Jess said. "We've always decorated a tree on Christmas Eve. I don't see why we should change that tradition."

"Oh, honey." Thomas glanced back toward the kitchen. "I don't know if this is a good idea."

Jess quickly kicked off her boots. "It's Christmas, Dad. Shouldn't Aaron and Kaylie be able to enjoy our old traditions? If Grandma were here, we'd be doing this tonight." She turned to Skyler and Rick. "Go get the old tree stand and Grandma's ornaments. We're going to decorate!"

Skyler stared at Rick and he stared back. Sly smiles spread slowly across their faces. "Let's go," Rick said. The two raced upstairs to retrieve the boxes of ornaments from the closet as the kids laughed at them.

"What on earth is all the noise out here?" Florence said, coming out from the kitchen. The minute she saw the fresh tree, her expression turned hard. She eyed Jess. "What is this about?"

"It's Christmas Eve, Mom. We're going to decorate a real tree like we used to."

Florence crossed her arms and glared at Jess, but to her credit, she didn't get angry in front of the children. "I'd like to see you in the kitchen," she told Jess.

"Fine." Jess glanced at Jay a moment, who shrugged, then followed her mother into the warm kitchen, letting the door swing closed behind her.

Florence spun on her heel the moment the door shut. "Why are you trying to ruin everyone's Christmas? We have a tree. Why can't you just let it be?"

Jess took a breath. "Mom, I honestly didn't bring it to upset you. Decorating a tree on Christmas Eve has always been our family tradition. I don't understand why you want to throw those things away."

"Throw them away?" Florence's face turned red with anger. "I'm not tossing anything away. But sometimes, it's just nice to let things be. That's something you obviously don't understand."

Jess frowned. "Me? You're the one who's been all over everyone, trying to tell them what to do with their lives. You won't let Skyler live her own life, and you've never stopped nagging me about Elaina. You're the one who doesn't understand how to let things be."

Florence's shoulders dropped, and she sat down in a kitchen chair. When she spoke, she sounded defeated. "You really don't get it, do you? It hurts to see your grandma's things. It reminds me that she's gone. I lost my best friend the day my mother died. It's so hard."

Jess had never seen her mother so vulnerable. It made her uncomfortable. She sat in the chair opposite her. "I miss grandma too. She and I were close. But seeing her things make me happy, not sad."

"I guess we're different that way," Florence said.

"You know, I lost my best friend the day Elaina died. So, I know how you feel," Jess said.

Florence looked up at her. "I'm sorry. I hadn't thought of it that way. She was your sister, but I didn't realize how close you two were."

"Sometimes it felt like you didn't know any of us," Jess said sadly.

Her mother dropped her head. "Grandma June and I were so close, it never occurred to me that I wouldn't be close with my own daughters. Maybe it was because I had four children instead of just one. Or maybe I didn't know how to connect with children. I was so busy running a house, working at the store, and taking care of you kids that I didn't have time to analyze it. I just did what I had to do."

Jess thought about that a moment. Her mother had been very busy when they were growing up. She'd just assumed her mother didn't make time for them. But the truth was, she didn't have extra time to spend with them.

"It really upset me when Elaina decided to go so far away for college," Florence continued. "I wanted to stay near my parents. But she wanted more than anything to get away." She looked directly at Jess. "Like you. You couldn't get out of here fast enough after high school."

"I couldn't stay after losing Elaina," Jess said. "I was constantly reminded that you thought it was my fault."

"What?" Florence stared at her, stunned.

"I knew you blamed me for the accident. That's why I wanted to leave."

"I never blamed you for the accident," Florence said. "I've always known it was my fault."

Jess was totally taken aback. "What? How could it have been your fault?"

"Elaina and I had a fight that afternoon before she ran out

and drove away. She was distracted because we'd fought over her going to California for college." Florence shook her head. "I shouldn't have pushed her. I should have been happy for her. Then we'd still have her here with us now."

"Wait." Jess was completely thrown off balance by her mother's confession. "I thought you blamed me. You've been hounding me for twenty years about what happened that day in the car."

"Oh, honey. I wasn't blaming you. I needed to know why it happened. If Elaina had been distracted because of me, I wanted to know." Florence's face softened. "But since you would never tell me, I figured it was my fault, and you didn't want me to know that."

Jess felt like she was living in an alternate universe. How could she believe one thing all these years and her mother believe another? It made no sense. "Why didn't you just tell me you blamed yourself? I would have told you it wasn't."

"I don't know. I didn't want you to know what I was thinking, I guess. I thought you hated me all those years because it was my fault," Florence said.

"Hated you? I've never hated you. We didn't always get along, but that was because we're both so stubborn—" Jess paused. "Oh no. Dad and Jay were right. You and I are exactly alike." She didn't know whether to laugh or cry.

"What? You and me? We're nothing alike," Florence said with certainty.

Jess laughed. "We are. We're both so stubborn that neither of us would open up and tell the other what we were thinking. Instead, we believed what we wanted to. And all it's done is cause a rift in our relationship all these years."

Her mother frowned, and Jess could tell she was thinking

about it. Finally, Florence looked up at her. "I think you're right." She actually smiled. "Boy, would your grandmother love this. She told me more than once that if I'd stop being so stubborn, maybe I'd find my answers."

Both women laughed in spite of themselves. After a moment, Jess reached over and touched her mother's hand. "If it will help ease your guilt, I'll tell you what happened that day in the car. It's hard, though. I don't like thinking about it."

"Please? I need to know," Florence said.

Jess took a deep breath and let it out slowly. "I was in the living room, sitting on the couch, when I heard you two fighting that day. I couldn't hear the exact words, but I figured it was about her choice of college. Then, Elaina came rushing out of the kitchen."

"Come on, Jess. Let's go for a drive." Elaina was wearing cut-off jean shorts, sneakers, and a tank top because there had been an unexpected hot spell that weekend. She was flushed from her tense conversation with their mother and had run out of the kitchen and grabbed Jess's hand. They slipped into her yellow Ford Mustang, blasted the stereo, and drove off.

"I can't wait to get out of this town," Elaina said. Her window was wide open, and her long blond hair floated all around her.

"I'll miss you, though," Jess told her. *"It'll just be me and the younger kids left, so basically me against Mom. She has the other two under her thumb."*

"You'll always have Grandma on your side," Elaina said. *"And besides. It's only two years. Then you can apply to Berkeley and come live with me and go to college. We'll be roommates again."* She smiled over at Jess, showing her perfectly straight teeth.

"I'd like that," Jess said.

Elaina snapped open the middle compartment and pulled out a pack of Salems. "Light one up for me, okay?" She handed them to Jess.

"Mom would like this," Jess said with a grin, and both girls laughed.

By now, they were out of town, speeding down the long, straight stretch of highway that separated the corn fields. Jess used the car's cigarette lighter to light a Salem and handed it to Elaina.

"Mom would kill you if she knew you smoked," Jess said.

"Mom doesn't approve of anything we do," Elaina said, laughing. "She's so uptight. Here," she handed Jess the cigarette. "Take a puff."

Jess did and started coughing. The menthol burned her lungs. "How can you stand these?" she asked.

Elaina laughed. "Lightweight. You get used to them."

Jess handed her the cigarette, and her sister took a long drag on it. Normally, Elaina was the perfect daughter, but Jess secretly liked her better when she was being herself. It meant she was human.

Elaina reached down and turned the music up louder. "I love this song!" Avril Lavigne was singing her new song, "Complicated." Elaina and Jess started moving and singing to the music, being silly.

Ashes fell off the cigarette and onto Elaina's seat. "Crap! Dad will kill me if I burn a hole in this seat," Elaina said, and both girls were laughing as they tried to wipe the hot ashes off the seat.

Jess glanced up and saw the four-way stop. "Elaina! Stop!" she yelled. Everything went black.

"The next thing I remember is waking up in the hospital," Jess said, tears filling her eyes. "We never saw the truck coming."

"Oh, sweetie." Florence was crying too.

"It was exactly as I've always said," Jess said. "A stupid teenage mistake. But afterward, when I learned Elaina had died, I swore I'd never tell anyone what had happened."

"Why?" her mother asked, wiping her tears with the back of her hand.

"Because it sounds like I'm blaming Elaina for the accident. And I didn't want anyone to think she died from a stupid mistake. She was so smart and had so much potential. I looked up to her. I didn't want people to think less of her. It was better to let them think I'd done something to distract her." Tears ran down Jess's cheeks. Florence grabbed a box of tissues from the counter and handed them to her.

"I never believed you caused the accident," Florence told Jess. "All these years, I thought she was distracted because of our argument."

"But what about all our fights? And why did you leave our room exactly the same all these years? I thought you did that to remind me of the accident," Jess said.

Florence's face fell. "Oh, no. After Elaina died, I was mad at myself and the world. I think you and I fought more because I couldn't cope with everything. And I left your room the same all these years to remind myself of what I'd done. I swear it wasn't to upset you."

Jess saw her mother in a new light. Of course, she'd struggled with losing her eldest daughter. But Jess had been so wrapped up in her own grief that she'd never thought about how her mother felt. "I'm sorry I didn't understand how you felt all those years ago, Mom. Grandma kept telling me you needed time, but I didn't understand then. I only cared about how Elaina's death had changed my life."

Florence gave her a small smile. "Sweetie, you were so young. How could you understand? And I should have been more sympathetic to your feelings. I'm sorry."

"We really are a pair, aren't we?" Jess asked. "All these years wasted being angry and feeling guilty. It's crazy."

Her mother walked over and wrapped her arms around Jess. It was the first real hug Jess and her mother had shared in over twenty years. All the years of anger melted away. "I'm glad we finally talked it out. Maybe we can both finally let it go."

Jess pulled back and smiled. "I'd like that."

A scream sounded out from the living room, and both Florence and Jess jumped. They flew out the door to find Skyler staring at a small red box in her hand.

"I found it!" Skyler yelled. "Grandma June's Christmas necklace. It was here all along."

Florence and Jess drew closer. "Where did you find it?" Florence asked. "I'd looked everywhere."

"It was right here," Skyler said. "In with the Christmas decorations. Grandma must have placed it in here the Christmas before she passed. She probably thought we'd be sure to find it here."

Florence shook her head. "And then I didn't use them for the past three years. How could I not have known this is where she'd leave the necklace? Your grandmother loved Christmas."

Jess gently squeezed her mother's arm. "There's no way you could have known. But at least we have it now."

Skyler tipped the box back and forth in the light. The silver star sparkled each time it hit the light. She turned and handed the box to her mother. "Now you can wear it each year, Mom."

"No," Florence said softly. She lifted the necklace from the box. "This necklace now belongs to the eldest granddaughter."

She turned and handed it to Jess. "Your grandma would want you to have it."

"Me?" Jess's eyes widened. "But it should be yours first, Mom."

Florence shook her head. "No. This necklace was always supposed to go to you. You and Grandma were very close. It's yours."

Jess looked uncertain. She glanced over at Skyler, but her sister nodded her approval.

"Just remember," Florence said. "It's up to you now to tell the story of Grandma June and Grandpa Pat's first Christmas. That honor comes with the necklace."

Tears filled Jess's eyes. That had always been her favorite part of Christmas Eve. "I will."

Jay walked over to Jess. "Can I help you put it on?"

She nodded and pulled her hair aside while Jay clasped the necklace.

"If Grandpa Pat were here, we all know what he'd say," Thomas said, smiling. "Everything is as it should be."

Florence nodded as she wiped away tears. "Well." She tried to sound more matter-of-fact. "The tree looks like it's shaping up nicely. Let's get the food on the table, and then we'll decorate it after dinner."

"Just as we've always done," Skyler said with a smile.

Jess nodded. "Just as we've always done." She glanced over at Jay, and he smiled back. It was going to be a wonderful Christmas after all.

CHAPTER SEVENTEEN

November 2019

June's coughing was growing worse. She hadn't felt well for quite some time, but she'd only thought it was an early winter cold. Every time Florence told her she should see a doctor, she'd brush it off. June knew her daughter was concerned, but it was just a cough. June didn't want to make a fuss over it.

June was looking forward to Christmas. She hadn't seen Jess since last Christmas, and she missed her granddaughter. She adored Skyler, of course, and her beautiful great-grandchildren, Aaron and now baby Kaylie, who'd just recently come into the world. And Rick and Mandy were always fun to visit with. She prayed daily for them to have the child they longed for. But still, June had been missing Jess the most.

Ever since losing her beloved Patrick two years ago, June's loneliness had grown deeper. She had her family around her, which she knew she was lucky for, but he was her other half, and she missed him dearly. She also hadn't been feeling as well over the past year. Her memory was not as sharp, and her movements were slower. More and more, June's mind wandered, and she thought of the past. How fast the years had gone. Too fast.

After Florence had left for work that day, June placed her Christmas necklace in its red box and went upstairs where they stored the ornaments. She was afraid with her fading memory she might lose her necklace before Christmas. June was determined to make sure that didn't happen.

Pulling the string on the overhead light in the storage closet, June rummaged around the room until she saw the clear bucket where her ornaments were now stored. It was much safer than the old box she'd once used and easier to find. Florence always placed the ornament bucket on the top of the pile so they wouldn't get damaged.

June carefully opened the bucket's lid and rummaged through it. On top was the beautiful tree topper she'd bought on sale at the dime store the day after Christmas in 1959. Below that was a box of Shiny Brite flocked round balls that she'd bought their first year together. June smiled as she looked at the red Merry Christmas ball and the blue Silent Night one. They looked just as beautiful as they had sixty years ago when they'd hung on their first tree. She loved thinking of each Christmas she and Pat shared and the ones with little Flori. They'd desperately wanted more children to share their lives with, but that never happened. After several miscarriages, Pat had begged June for them to stop trying, especially after she'd almost bled to death. Finally, she agreed, and he'd had a vasectomy so there was no chance of ever facing another disappointing miscarriage. But even to this day, June grieved not having more children.

Still, her life was filled with grandchildren and great-grandchildren, and for that she was grateful.

June placed her necklace box in the bottom of the ornament

container and then stacked the others on top. Carefully, she snapped the lid back on. "Now I won't forget my necklace. It'll be here, waiting for me on Christmas Eve."

Slowly, June turned off the light and left the storage room. At the top of the stairs, she stopped and began coughing. Her chest hurt from the deep rumble of her cough. Maybe Florence was right. She should go in soon to see the doctor if the cough didn't go away.

Carefully, she made her way down the stairs. Perhaps a cup of tea with honey and a short nap would help her feel better. As June put the kettle on the stove and pulled down one of her old China teacups, she smiled. She couldn't wait for Christmas.

Five days later, June passed away in the hospital from pneumonia.

CHAPTER EIGHTEEN

New Year's Eve 2022

Jess stayed on through the next week instead of going home. She wanted to spend time with her mother, so they could get to know each other again. Jess also wanted to work with Skyler on her divorce and make sure it was what her sister wanted.

And on a personal note, Jess wanted to spend more time with Jay. He'd already proven to her he was interested, and she was drawn to him as she had been in high school. But she wanted to see if her feelings were real or if she was just reminiscing about her younger years.

"It's real," Jay told her two nights after Christmas as they sat curled up in front of his fireplace. "At least for me, it is. You know," he glanced down at his lap, looking suddenly shy. "I never stopped caring about you."

"Really?" Jess was shocked. "But we broke up before leaving for college. And you married someone else."

"You broke up with me before leaving for college," he reminded her. "And yes, I was married, but she and I never had the easy relationship you and I had. That's why it didn't work."

Jess studied his face. She still knew him well and could tell he was being sincere. "I broke up with you so you'd be free to move on with your life. I was too self-absorbed then. I wanted to prove myself to my family and get over losing Elaina. And we were just kids."

He gave her a small smile. "We're not kids anymore."

"No, we're not," she said. "But I'm still trying to figure things out."

"Well, we can be friends until you do," he said, holding her hand.

His words had left Jess rethinking her life. Was she happy living in Minneapolis and working for that large firm? She knew better than anyone that divorce rates were high when high school sweethearts married. But what if you got back together years later?

Her mother posed the same question as they cleaned out Jess and Elaina's childhood room and packed up the old trophies and mementos. "You and Jay have been spending a lot of time together. Is there something there?"

Jess shrugged. "I'm not sure. I still feel close to him, but can we really have a relationship after all these years?"

"Anything's possible," Florence said. "Look at us."

This made Jess laugh. "That's true." She picked up Elaina's senior picture. "Where do you want this?"

Florence took it from her and gazed at it lovingly. "I think on the shelves downstairs where my mom and dad's photos are. I can look at it now and remember the happy times."

"I think that's a great idea," Jess said. She was glad her mother was no longer tormenting herself over Elaina's death. They were both at peace with it.

That week they moved one of the twin beds into Skyler's old

room for when her kids stayed over and placed the other twin bed in the storage room. Then her mother bought a queen-size bed, and Jess helped her pick out new curtains and a bedspread for the room. Everything still matched the old flowered wallpaper Grandma June had put in the room decades ago, but it now looked more like a guest room. And Jess appreciated not having to sleep on a small bed anymore.

"Are you ready to go through grandma and grandpa's room yet?" Jess asked her mother. "I'll help you if you are."

Florence shook her head. "Not yet. But when I do, I'll have you and Skyler do it with me, and we'll let Rick pick a few things he'd like, too."

"That sounds good," Jess said.

As New Year's Eve approached, Jay asked Jess if she'd like to come to The Pier to celebrate. "Half the town will be there," he said. "But mostly, I want you there."

"I'd like to be there with you," she told him. "But I should spend it with the family. After that, I'll have to go home."

He nodded. "Okay. But if you get a chance, come over and we can have a glass of champagne."

She wished now that her mother wasn't making a big deal over New Year's Eve, but she didn't want to disappoint her by not being there.

The day before New Year's Eve, Jess stopped by Mandy's hair salon to check on her. Mandy had an hour before her next client, so they went across the street to the sandwich shop and ate lunch.

"How are you feeling?" Jess asked. She couldn't speak freely in front of her parents and Skyler, so she wanted to talk to her privately.

"A little crazy with the hormones, but that will be over

soon," Mandy said with a sly smile.

"Why? You're not giving up, are you?"

"No, not at all. In fact, I'm scheduled for the egg implant on January fourth. Wish us luck. We only have one more frozen egg left after this, and I'm not sure I have enough energy to try this again," Mandy said.

Jess grabbed her hands across the table. "I know it'll be successful this time," she told her. "I'll only think happy thoughts for you both that day."

Mandy smiled. "We'll need it. But this is all hush, hush, okay? If it doesn't work, I don't want anyone else to know."

Jess nodded. Some secrets were necessary to keep your sanity.

"Did you two sneak off for lunch without me?" Skyler stood by the table, giving them a pouty look.

Jess laughed. "Yep. Just like old times. We left the bratty little sister behind."

Skyler looked startled a moment before she realized Jess was teasing her. "Can I join you two?"

"Of course." Jess scooted over in the booth to give her room to sit. "We were just catching up. It's hard to talk when every-one is at the house."

"That's for sure," Skyler said. She smiled over at Mandy. "You look great today. You're practically glowing."

"Really? Thanks," Mandy said. "Maybe it's because I'm happy. You and Jess are here, and the family is finally getting along. It's been a long time coming."

"Yes, it has," Skyler said. "And despite everything going on with Chris and me, I'm actually really happy too. It's like the weight of the world has been lifted off me. Or at least a hundred and ninety extra pounds." She giggled.

Jess turned serious. "So, you're absolutely sure this is what you want? No couples therapy or anything first?"

"It is what I want," Skyler said. "I've been worrying about my marriage for several months now, and I'm done with it. I'm relieved. And so is Chris. We talked the other night, and he said he was glad he was no longer lying to me. He said he'd be reasonable about the divorce and do everything he can to stay close to the kids. I couldn't ask for anything more than that."

"Wow," Jess said. "What came over him? The Spirit of Christmas?"

Skyler laughed. "I'm not sure. Maybe he had a Scrooge moment or something. But I'm feeling really good about it."

"I'm happy for you," Mandy said. "You can move on with your life and have the chance to find happiness again."

"You mean like Jess." Skyler slid her eyes to her sister. "Jess and Jay, sitting in a tree."

"Oh, stop!" Jess said. "Just because I've spent a lot of time with Jay doesn't mean anything is happening. I have a whole life in Minneapolis."

"But you don't have Jay there," Skyler said. "Or me, or Mandy, or Rick, or your niece and nephew. When are you going to realize you belong here with all of us?"

Jess laughed. "In this little town? What would I do? Put together crop contracts and write up wills? I don't think there are enough divorces to keep an office open."

"You could do plenty of legal work around here. You just have to be creative," Skyler said. "I miss having you around."

"I miss family too when I'm not here," Jess said. Even with the problems she'd had with her mother in the past, Jess had missed the camaraderie of her sister and Mandy all these years.

The three talked, laughed, and teased throughout lunch,

and Jess enjoyed every minute of it. She knew she'd miss this once she went home. The life waiting for her was boring and serious. Most of her friends were women she worked with, and they were always conscious of their positions in the firm. She never met men like Jay, either. Most men were intimidated by her the second they learned she was a lawyer. And dating a lawyer was out of the question. She'd tried that once, and it hadn't ended well. He'd treated their relationship like a competition, and she'd been exhausted by it. But move back to Redmond? Jess wasn't sure about that, either.

On New Year's Eve, everyone came over to the house and her mother cooked a big meal. They undecorated the tree and carefully put away Grandma June's old ornaments while reminiscing about past holidays. It didn't feel like work; it was fun to do it together, and it didn't leave a mess for their mother to clean up alone.

Once everyone was filled with food and cake for dessert and the tree was out of the house, they all started to leave. Skyler was the first to go because the kids were falling asleep despite wanting to stay up until midnight. Then Mandy and Rick left, both too tired from working that day to hang on until the new year.

"Well, it looks like it's just the three of us," Jess said as she helped her mother take the last of the dessert plates into the kitchen.

"Don't count on your father," Florence said. "He'll be asleep in his chair by the time we're done in here."

Jess laughed. She peeked out the kitchen door and sure enough, her father was already snoring.

"Isn't there a New Year's party over at The Pier tonight?" Florence asked. "I'm sure Jay would enjoy it if you showed up."

Jess yawned, then chuckled. "I doubt I'd make it until midnight," she said. "How about a game of Scrabble before bed?"

She and her mother sat at the dining room table playing Scrabble with the TV on low, showing a New Year's Eve count-down show in New York City. By eleven-thirty, Florence shook Thomas awake, and he stumbled off to bed.

"I'm glad you stayed an extra week," Florence told Jess. "This was fun. Sorry we're old party poopers, though."

"I'm glad I stayed too. I wouldn't be doing anything fun at my house. This was nice," Jess said.

Her mother hugged her goodnight and followed Thomas upstairs to bed. With nothing else to do, Jess turned off the downstairs lights and went up to her newly decorated room.

Looking out the window, she watched the stars sparkle in the big open sky. Jess put on her old color-block jacket, wrapped a blanket around her, then opened the window and sat on the ledge with her feet on the roof. She took a deep breath of the crisp air and thought nothing had ever felt so good. She was home, where she belonged. And for the first time in years, she really felt she belonged here.

A noise against the roof startled her, and Jess looked down to see Jay climbing up the old ladder.

"Are you crazy?" she said softly so as not to wake her parents.

Jay's head popped up over the rim of the roof, and he grinned. "Haven't I always been a little crazy?" He carefully walked up the steep roof to the window and sat down beside her. "You're not up here smoking those weird cigarettes again, are you?"

"No. I was enjoying the peace and quiet of the night."

"I thought you were celebrating with your parents and

family," Jay said.

"They all gave up early," Jess said. "I figured I'd meet the new year up here under the stars."

"Not a bad idea." Jay smiled and his eyes twinkled as he pulled a bottle out of one pocket and two champagne glasses out of the other.

"Aren't you supposed to be at your bar hosting a party?" Jess asked. She was actually glad he'd come up here with her.

"They can drink and do the countdown without me," he said. "Here, hold these while I open this bottle."

"Champagne?" she asked. "And plastic glasses?"

"I couldn't risk them breaking in my pocket," he said. He took off the foil and then fought with the top. It popped off and flew over to the roof of his house. They both jumped at the noise and then laughed.

"Don't wake up my parents," she said in a mock whisper.

"Wouldn't be the first time," he replied.

They sat there sipping champagne and enjoying the peaceful night. Jess couldn't help but lean against Jay because the window ledge was so small, and she didn't mind it. Finally, he turned to her.

"So, after all this, you're going back to Minneapolis to continue your life as usual?" Jay asked.

Jess shrugged. "What else would I do? It's not like I have a lot of options."

At that moment, the church bells began to ring. The new year had arrived.

Jay looked at Jess and lifted his glass. "Happy New Year."

She touched her glass to his and smiled. "Happy New Year."

Jay reached over and drew Jess to him, kissing her softly on the lips before pulling away slightly. It had been decades since they'd kissed, yet all the magic was still there. Jess didn't want him to stop. Reaching her arms up around his neck, she kissed him with a passion that surprised them both.

Jay was the first one to pull away. He smiled at her, his blue eyes dancing. "So, about those options," he said.

Jess laughed, then gave in to his kiss once more.

EPILOGUE

Christmas Eve 2023

Jess stood decorating the Christmas tree as Jay carefully unpacked ornaments from the container. Aaron and Kaylie begged to help as Skyler cautioned them not to break the antique ornaments. Thomas watched all the craziness from his comfortable chair, and Florence and Mandy had just come out of the kitchen from cleaning up after dinner. Rick was just coming downstairs with another box of decorations, and the kids made a beeline for him.

"Can we help?" six-year-old Aaron asked hopefully. Four-year-old Kaylie jumped up and down next to her brother. "Please?"

Rick let out a loud belly laugh, and everyone shushed him at once.

"You'll wake the baby," Florence said, looking into the infant carrier at her three-month-old granddaughter. "Oh, little June is so cute," Florence gushed.

Jess smiled over at Mandy, still thrilled that the IVF had worked and Rick and Mandy were now parents. Skyler had been happy for them too. Now her kids would have a cousin to play with in the next few years. But of everyone, Florence was the happiest. She adored being a grandmother and had been warmed by the fact that they'd named their little girl after her mother, June.

The baby whimpered, and Mandy reached down and lifted her from the carrier. Florence hurried to the kitchen to warm a bottle. After setting down the ornaments, Rick came up beside Mandy. She handed him little June and the diaper bag.

"Daddy's turn to change the diaper," Mandy said, giving Rick a grin.

Rick didn't mind. He slung the bag over his shoulder and carried the baby to June and Patrick's old bedroom, which now was set up with a changing table and toys for the children. Once Florence learned that she would be a grandmother again, she decided to make the change and turn the old bedroom into a playroom.

"It'll be perfect for when everyone is here," Florence had told Jess as they cleaned out the room along with Skyler. "The kids can have their toys in here, and it won't matter if it's a mess. Grandma June loved children. She'd be pleased this room is now a playroom."

Jess had agreed. Her Grandma June would have loved to have been here with the children all around.

Now, as she stood by the tree, Jess touched the Christmas star charm that hung around her neck. Grandma June would be pleased about many things that had happened this year. She could practically feel her smiling down on them.

Three months after the new year, Jess had decided she'd had enough of her life as a divorce attorney and made the move home. She and Jay had continued their relationship, although it was difficult being four hours away from each other. Jess quit her job and sold her townhouse and hadn't looked back. Her intention was to start her own practice in Redmond and buy a small house of her own. But after living with her parents for six weeks—spending most of her free time at Jay's house—she gave in to the fact that she wanted to live with Jay. He'd invited her to live with him months before, but she had to make sure she was ready. By May, she was, and they'd been happily living together since.

Jess had rented the last open space next door to Mandy's salon—from her parents, of course—and turned it into an office. She'd hired a nice young woman as a secretary, who'd been happy to find a good job in such a small town, and opened her doors. Surprisingly, Jess was busy immediately, and her business had grown over the months. She still worked on divorces, though rarely. Mostly, she did wills and contracts and a whole hodgepodge of other legal things that people needed in a small town. It wasn't hard work or high stress, and she loved that. She could close the office doors at five every night and have her weekends off. Weekends she spent with Jay whenever he could get away from The Pier.

Rick returned with the freshly diapered baby and Florence claimed her. She sat in the old rocking chair that had once belonged to Grandma June's mother and rocked gently as she fed little June her bottle. Florence was happy and content with this new little bundle she could spoil and love.

"We have news," Mandy said, looking around at everyone. All eyes turned to her.

"You're not pregnant again?" Skyler asked, looking shocked.

Mandy laughed. "No. Definitely not. Remember when Rick and I signed up to possibly adopt a child? We received a call yesterday that there is a two-year-old little boy who needs a home. We are already approved to be a foster family, so we could take him immediately."

Everyone stared at her with wide eyes. Jess broke the silence. "Are you going to bring him home?"

Mandy nodded her head, smiling. "Yes. We're picking him up the day after tomorrow. If everything works out, we'll have another child in the family."

Rick sat down next to Mandy and held her hand. "We're really excited about this," he said. "We're hoping that all of you will treat him as if he's our own."

Jess smiled wide. "Are you kidding? Of course, we will!" She went over and hugged Mandy and then her brother. "I can't wait to welcome him into the family."

"Me, too," Florence said. "I couldn't be happier for you both. You're going to be very busy with two little ones, but that's what having a family is about."

Everyone hugged Mandy and Rick. They were all happy to welcome a new child into their midst.

"And I'll help out whenever I can," Skyler said excitedly. "The kids would love to have playdates with another little cousin." Her divorce had been finalized earlier in the year and Skyler had purchased a cute little three-bedroom home right down the block from her parents' house. She'd told Jess that she actually preferred the smaller house to the big one on the lake. It was easier to care for and was close to the park so she and the kids could walk there on summer evenings. And the children could see their grandparents more often, too.

"We'll all help," Jess said. "At this rate, we should open a Day Care Center on our side of the block downtown." She laughed until she noticed everyone staring at her. "Oh, no. I'm